FACE YOUR FEARS

Robert Campbell

Published by Robert Campbell

The characters and events portrayed in this book are fictitious. Any similarity to real persons, living or dead, is coincidental and not intended by the author.

Cover design by: Chris Meeks
Printed in the United States of America

ACKNOWLEDGEMENTS

Thank you to my family who has supported me through this dream, Renee Gordon, my editor, who keeps me on my toes and Chris Meeks for my awesome cover.

CONTENTS

CHAPTER 1

Halloween is finally here, and I couldn't be any more excited! This year I'm going to be the Grim Reaper. My Grim Reaper costume came in last week from Amazon. It has a black hood a skull mask and glowing red eyes. I'm happy with it. All week long, I've been preparing for tonight when I would scare all the little kids and take their candy from them. All mine--it's all going to be mine!

I took some aluminum foil and wrapped it around a piece of cardboard I cut out to make my sickle. Once I finished with that, I placed it on the broom handle that I'd spray-painted black. It was perfect if I do say so myself. Those little brats will run scared tonight.

My name is Brendan and I'm a bully. I'm the kid who picks on other kids. I don't know why I do it, I just do. I'm bigger than the average twelve-year-old so that's one of the reasons why I get away with it. Most kids just run away scared of me. I like it. I like it a lot actually.

Last week my best friend Derek and I took stuttering Pete to the bathroom and stuck his head into the toilet, giving him a class-A swirly. I got detention for it, which was nothing. I hit Mr. Wheeler on top of his shiny bald head with a spit wad when his back was turned. Everyone in detention got a good laugh out of it. Everyone except Mr. Wheeler, that is. My parents say they don't know what to do with me. They just don't understand why I act the way I do. It's not that they're not good parents or anything, I just like being who I am. I honestly don't have an answer for them. My dad told me one day I was going to pick on the wrong person. That it wasn't going to matter how big I was or how little they were, that person would get the best of me. Yeah, that still hasn't happened.

I looked outside and saw that the sun was starting to set slowly behind the clouds. The wind was picking up and I watched as the leaves swirled across the sidewalk. My neighbors had their yard decorated with all kinds of Halloween decorations. There was a witch that looked like she crashed into the telephone pole, a couple of well-placed carved pumpkins on the porch that soon would be lit on the inside with candles. A scarecrow sitting on a hay bale and ghosts hanging from the trees completed the look. They always go all out. My parents, on the other hand, not so much. We just carve pumpkins. My dad doesn't care much for Halloween. He's what you would call a class-A nerd. Mom says he was picked on a lot in school, but she was attracted to him for his brain. He's intelligent she says.

When we were younger mom would sit down and watch horror movies with my sister and me. We would eat popcorn and sip on root beer floats all night. Not anymore. She stays busy at the office a lot. I finished trying on my costume one more time and put the mask on. Yep, Brendan, you sure outdid yourself this time. I heard my door open. I turned and looked over my shoulder. It was my mother.

"Brendan, honey, I need to ask you for a favor son." "Ok, mom what is it," I answered back.

"I need you to take your sister to the fall festival tonight for Halloween and then maybe around the block of the neighborhood afterward depending on if she gets enough prizes or not."

I took a deep breath and thought about my next words. This was Halloween, my favorite holiday that only happens once a year.

"Mom, why do I have to take her? You're supposed to do that, not me! I've made plans with Derek! We're supposed to meet up at his house for a Halloween party. Please don't make me do this," I pleaded with her.

"Honey, your dad has to go away on business. He got the call twenty minutes ago. I have to take him to the airport for his flight but beforehand we're going into town to get something to eat, so we're leaving you in charge. You're old enough to be responsible now, and that means watching your sister when we ask you to.

You're going to have to call Derek and tell him you can't make it this year. I'm so sorry son."

"Ok, fine! I'll take the little snot-nose brat to the school festival and around the block to trick or treat," I said.

"Brendan your sister's not a brat and you're the eldest and you could protect her. Plus, she looks up to you Brendan if you hadn't noticed lately. So, I expect you to be home at a decent hour."

"Ok" was all I could say at this point.

My mom walked out with a smile and shut the door behind her. What a waste of a year I thought to myself. All this build-up for nothing to take my sister, the snot nose princess, to the festival. I guess this is the price you pay for being a bully. I could still have a little fun. I don't have to let my sister ruin it for me. I could still snag a bag or two and have the brat help me. We both would come out well in the end. I would have more candy and so would she. It sounded good to me. All of a sudden, I heard my sister's loud scream from upstairs.

I heard my mom and dad rush upstairs. She screamed again this time even louder than the first. I hurried up the stairs nearly tripping on my skateboard I left out in the hallway. I climbed up the stairs and made my way to my sister's door. I opened it and saw that my mother was trying to calm her down. Emma's face was covered in tears. Then I heard the voice speak "Emma! Emma! I'm coming to get you."

Emma tucked her head deep into mother's shoulder. I tried not to laugh but couldn't help it. My trick worked. I scared my sister with my tape recorder.

"This isn't funny at all Brendan." My mother said impatiently.

I watched as my mother dug through my sister's closet. She found the voice recorder behind my sister's jewelry box. I figured it would be a less suspecting spot to put it. A deep voice sounded from behind me, "Brendan I told you what would happen if you teased your sister again."

I turned around. It was my father. He was wiping the sweat off his bald head with a napkin. He was gasping for breath from running up the stairs so quickly.

"Brendan, I want your Xbox and your Blu-ray player right now. Go get it for me," my father ordered me.
"Dad, seriously," I spluttered.

My dad didn't say another word and I could tell he meant it. He wasn't backing down. I walked out of my sister's room stomping my feet down the stairs. I opened the door to my room where I was greeted by whiskers our big grey cat. He was laying on my bed like he always does. I unplugged both my Xbox and Blu-ray player and walked back upstairs where my father was waiting on me to 'hand it over' as he would say.

"Hand it over son."

I didn't argue, I just did it. He turned and left my sister's room. He took my electronics to his bedroom, and I heard him lock the door behind him as he came back out.

"Brendan, I do hope someday you will grow out of these foolish antics of yours and see that there's more to life than bullying people the way you do," my father said.

"Now listen to me son, I better not hear your sister say anything about you scaring her or anyone else for that matter. I hear one bad report from her, and your punishment will be worse than just your electronics being taken. Do I make myself clear Brendan?"

"Yes, sir," was all I could say.

I watched as my father walked out of my sister's room and went downstairs to finish getting ready.

My mother was fixing my sister's hair. Emma was going to be the Disney princess Snow White. She looked the part too. My sister was always so perfect, she couldn't do anything wrong. I call her the brat because of it. She hates that nickname, so I keep using it just because I know it annoys her.

I walked downstairs and sat down on the couch to wait for my sister so I could take her to the fall festival. My mother and father came downstairs shortly behind me. My mother turned and looked at me.

"Remember Brendan no more tricks and be home early. I better not hear anything else more about you playing tricks on her."

"Yes, mother," I answered.

My dad helped my mother into her coat, and they walked out the door. Thirty minutes later my sister Emma came downstairs in her Snow-White costume ready to go.

"I'm ready," she said as she turned towards me. I opened the door and we walked out into the night together.

We made our way outside our home into the cold night air. The school was a few blocks from the house. The neighbor's yard was lit up with pumpkins and there was corny Halloween music playing. A fog machine sat in the corner with a strobe light set up beside it. The skeleton's shadows appeared to be dancing on the wall as the wind was blowing them. For a moment, they seemed to come to life.

My sister caught me dozing off as I was admiring the decorations. My sister shouted at me, "Come on Brendan we're going to be late!"

I caught up to her and we made our way down Cones Road the street we lived on. After five minutes of walking, we passed my friend Derek's house. I heard a door slam and watched as he ran towards our direction. Derrick called out to me, "Hey Brendan!"

I stopped to wait for him and watched as he almost tripped on a sprinkler head. Derek has always been clumsy. Once he tripped on his shoelace in Mrs. Epperson's class spilling her coffee all over her shirt as he knocked her over by her desk. The whole class erupted into laughter. It was funny, but not for Derek. He spent two weeks in detention for it. He tried to tell everyone he did it on purpose. He wasn't fooling anyone.

"Hey, Derek," I said.

"We still going out tonight to snatch the kid's candy?" he asked.

"I can't. My mother and father are out on a date. My dad has a business meeting out of town, so I got stuck taking the brat to the Fall Festival tonight so she can try to win some prizes. Then I gotta take her around the block to trick or treat."

Derek shook his head and laughed. "You must hate being the babysitter."

"Yes, it can be annoying. Sometimes I wish I was an only child because the brat is spoiled."

Emma punched me in the arm for my comment. She was ready to leave and getting impatient.

"Come on Brendan we're gonna miss all the cool prizes."

"We're gonna miss all the cool prizes," I said mockingly. Derek chimed in following my lead. We both teased Emma, mocking her dancing in the street for a second. I stopped finally, knowing I had to get her to the school and knowing also that she would tell my mom on me if I didn't take her.

"Derek I gotta go, I have to get her there tonight. Maybe we can do something later if my mom comes home early enough. I don't plan on being out all night with my sister at that silly Fall Festival."

"Ok, Brendan just call me later on tonight if you can."

I watched as Derek turned and ran back up the street towards his two-story home. His house looked creepy. The back windows looked like eyes peering down at Emma and me. I heard his door slam behind him, and we continued down the street walking towards the school. We'd be there in a few minutes. A few kids passed us dressed as ghosts, witches, and one zombie. I thought the zombie looked pretty cool with his painted pale skin and his eye that looked like it was dangling out of its socket.

Up ahead I could see the school with all the cars parked out front. Finally, I thought to myself, we're here! Now, if we can just hurry and get this over with so I can have some time to myself. We made our way inside. Let the festivities begin.

Emma rushed past me, knocking me into the brick wall. She was excited. She loved attending the Fall Festival. She looked forward to it every year. Her favorite event is the cakewalk. Last year she won a chocolate cake that was decorated like a pumpkin with ghosts painted on it. I saw our principal Mr. Harris. He was dressed as Batman. I thought it was silly of him, but he looked the part. Mr. Harris has a stocky build. He's tall with wide shoulders and big arms. He looks like a pro wrestler. He played college football as a defensive tackle until he broke his leg. He could have gone pro my dad once told me.

The cafeteria was crowded with people in their costumes. It's the one time of year you can be something different other than yourself. I spotted Mrs. Epperson in the crowd. She was dressed as Frankenstein's bride and was working the bobbing for apples station. I looked for Emma and finally found her waiting in line for the cakewalk event. I really didn't mind that she had gotten away from me earlier. We live in a small community where everyone knows everyone. I sat down at one of the cafeteria tables and watched her. It was her turn. The music played and she started walking in a circle with eight other people. Most of the kids were her age. One girl was dressed as Barbie and another little girl was dressed as a pumpkin. They marched for a few more times and Emma was eliminated. I could see the disappointment on her face as she walked towards me.

"Come on you can try another event," I said to her. Emma just groaned.

We walked towards the bobbing for apples station and Emma handed Mrs. Epperson her ticket.

I stood waiting patiently as Emma tried to bite into an apple and bring it back up from the water bucket. It was amusing to watch her try to hold her hair back to keep from getting it wet. It didn't work out too well for her. I giggled a little bit at her. On her last attempt, she came up with an apple in her mouth and everyone clapped. For her effort, she was awarded a large bag of candy. She rushed over to me, excited to show me the contents of her bag.

"Brendan! Look inside my bag, it's full of candy! I'm so excited!"

I humored her and peered inside her bag. It wasn't bad actually. It was filled with Whoppers, Tootsie Rolls, Starburst, and lots of other sweets to give her a sugar rush.

"Ok, Emma what do you wanna do next?" I asked her.

"Let's go to the dart game. The one where you throw the darts at the balloons."

We walked over to the dart booth and I handed Emma another

two tickets for the game. Our guidance counselor Mr. Johnson was dressed as a scarecrow. If you have ever seen him in person, you couldn't help but laugh at him. He has a big nose and a unibrow and he's obsessed with comic books, which isn't a bad thing since it's the latest popular trend now with all the movies coming out in theaters lately. I watched as Emma threw her first dart, which barely missed Mr. Johnson's hat.

"Sorry, Mr. Johnson." Everyone laughed at her.

I could tell Mr. Johnson wasn't amused. She threw her second one and hit her target. The balloon popped.
Mr. Johnson turned his back as Emma threw her third and final dart.

"Youch!" he yelled. Everyone pointed and laughed, including me. Emma had hit Mr. Johnson square in the butt with her final dart.

"I'm so sorry, Mr. Johnson. I didn't mean to...," she exclaimed.

"Emma just take your prize and don't come back to this stand tonight," Mr. Johnson replied.

Emma won a lava lamp for her trouble. Everyone was still laughing. Now, that made up for what I thought was going to be the worst night of my life. Emma had made me laugh.

"Well, Emma, I guess dart throwing is not in your near future." Emma just chuckled at my joke.

"Hey! Emma, Brendan!" a voice called out.

We both turned and looked over our shoulder. It was the pest, Staci, Emma's best friend. Staci can be incredibly annoying. Her voice is loud, and it carries. She's short and has big ears and long curly blond hair. Emma and Staci have been best friends the past two years ever since Staci moved to our district. Me, I'm just mean to her for no reason.

"Emma come on, I have an extra ticket for the hayride. I want you to go with me."

"Go ahead Emma, it'll be fun. I'll be waiting here for you.

“Emma hugged me and ran alongside her friend, while I had a great idea. I'm going to play a game. The name of the game is let's scare Staci. I grabbed some fake plastic spiders from a spider’s web, and I knew exactly what to do with them.

CHAPTER 2

I held the black plastic spiders in my hand and slipped outside eagerly to throw them on Staci. I watched as one of the parents, who seated them on a hay bale, greeted Emma and Staci. A few more kids got on the trailer that would soon be pulled by a John Deer tractor. The hayride was always the same. It hooks a left by the creek, then turns up the hill by the high school and lasts maybe twenty to thirty minutes. When I was Emma's age, I always enjoyed it. I snuck out quickly so no one could see me. I knew the perfect hiding spot - the bridge by the creek.

It was an excellent idea. After all, my costume is black and would conceal me well in the night. I flashed back to a memory of when I was younger and a bigger boy by the name of Ryan liked to pick on me. Five years ago, when I was smaller, he picked me up, carried me to the creek, and held my head underwater until I nearly passed out. I remember him and his friends running away, slapping high fives as they took my bag of candy and the prizes I had won. My costume was ruined that night and I remember that my elbow was gashed open. I told myself never again would I be the victim.

Since that day I've done everything I could to show people that I'm not a wimp. I built a reputation of being the kid the other kids don't want to upset. So far, it's worked out well for me. Now, I'm the size of Ryan or bigger and I would love to be able to get my hands on him someday, but that will never happen. Ryan moved out of town shortly after that. Good riddance was all I could say.

I could see the tractor coming. I still had a few minutes to get ready. One of the parents was telling a scary story, as they always do. Usually, it's the story about the headless horseman. You know, the story about the schoolteacher who went the wrong direction and was never seen again, and everyone claims it was the headless horseman. It's a classic.

I turned and looked at the tractor as it was making the loop around the gym. Soon I would scare those little brats. All of a sudden, I felt someone's cold hand touch the back of my neck. I jerked hard and smacked my elbow into the person behind me. I heard their breath leave them. I looked to see who had grabbed me and saw it was Derek. He was holding his stomach and grunting in pain.

"Dang Brendan, why did you do that!" he gasped.

"Sorry, Derek, but you shouldn't touch me from behind like that. I mean what did you think was going to happen?"

"I'm not sure, but I know I'll never do it again."

"I'm about to scare my sister and her friend Staci. I've got some plastic spiders, and I know she hates them, so if you wanna help then you gotta be quiet. They'll be here in a minute."

Derek just nodded his head. Derek was dressed as a werewolf. His mask looked almost real. There was fake blood dripping down the teeth and the hair was long black and grey. The yellow eye looked aggressive. He wore a red plaid shirt with black pants and fake claws on his fingers.

"Ok, here they come! Get ready."

I couldn't wait to jump the ride and see the look on their scared little faces. I'm glad Derek was here to help out because it made the prank twice as much fun. I watched as they rounded the corner.

"In 3...2...1..." I counted.

We jumped onto the back of the trailer and the kids screamed loudly. One of the parents fell off the trailer. I heard them hit the ground with a loud thud. Derek grabbed Emma as she screamed, terrified.

I grabbed Staci and the ride proceeded without them. Staci lay on the ground screaming. I grabbed the spiders and threw them on her. Staci went to kicking and trying to crawl away from the fake spiders. Derek had finally let up on Emma and I slapped him a high five as he approached where I was standing. We took off our masks and started laughing at Emma and Staci.

"You guys are such jerks!" Emma yelled.

I turned around and watched as she punched Derek hard in the stomach, knocking the wind out of him. Emma reached out her hand, helping Staci up and brushing her off. "I'm going home Brendan, and I will be telling mom about this." she scoffed at me. “Come on Staci, let’s go. Are you okay?”

"Emma it's okay, I'd rather walk by myself. Seriously, I'm fine."

"Staci, are you sure? I can walk you home." Emma answered.

Staci didn't answer. She just turned and left. Tears were still flowing down her face. Emma turned and stared me down, still angry at mine and Derek's prank.

"Brendan I'm leaving and going home. That prank was so wrong. You should have never done that to Staci. She didn't deserve it." Emma stomped off, making her way back to the school. I didn't say anything.

"Brendan, your brat sister is going home, so let's go steal some bags from the kids still trick or treating the neighborhood."

"Derek I can't, my mom and dad told me I need to stay out of trouble. If I don't take Emma trick or treating now, she will tell mom and dad what I did, and I don't need that right now. I gotta go and catch up with her." Derek just stared at me with a blank expression on his face.

The prank was fun, and the excitement was short-lived. Now I had to catch up with my sister if I could find her. I heard the motor of the tractor making its way back towards our direction. It was tempting to jump on and ride back, but I decided to run, as the school wasn't that far away.

"See ya' later Derek," I called out as I started to sprint.

I cut through the practice field where our senior high football team practiced. I couldn't wait to suit up one day in shoulder pads and helmet. I knew I would be a good athlete. Our senior football team was undefeated, and everyone said this was the year we would go to the state playoffs and hopefully win it. I had no doubt, when last Friday we won our home game. The other team didn't even score a touchdown on us. Our team was nothing less than awesome.

I could see the Elementary school in the distance. The parking lot was still full. Good, I thought. Now I had to find my bratty sister, Emma the terror. I beat the tractor here thanks to the shortcut across the ball field. I went inside and started to look for my sister. The crowd had grown in the short thirty to forty-five minutes I was absent. This wasn't going to be easy. I didn't want to ask Mr. Johnson where my sister was because I was sure he was still upset over the events that had transpired earlier with Emma and her horrible aim. Well, it was a nice shot I would say. It's not like Mr. Johnson didn't deserve it since he felt the need to keep me in detention all the time.

I made my way back towards his balloon booth. The line was long, but I didn't have time to just sit and wait.

"Mr. Johnson!" I called out. I'm not sure he heard me.

I fought my way up front knocking some older guy's soda on his costume. "Hey kid why don't you watch where you're going!" he yelled towards me.

I didn't have time to respond. "Mr. Johnson!"

He turned and looked over his shoulder at me. "What is it, Brendan? How can I assist you?"

"Have you seen Emma? I 'm looking for her."

"No, I have not seen her Brendan. If she's lost it means you need to do a better job at keeping an eye on her." He snapped at me.

I didn't say what I wanted. I didn't have time to argue or pick a fight with Mr. Johnson, besides everyone would be talking about what Emma did to him for the next few weeks and he would have the pleasure of not living it down. That was enough for me. I was satisfied with that thought.

I looked around, checking other games the kids were playing to see if Emma was standing in line and I had overlooked her. I looked at the basketball shot first. One kid actually made his first throw. I was impressed because he was so small, he looked like he could barely pick the ball up. He made his second shot. His parents cheered him on as he won a big bag of candy.

I still didn't see Emma anywhere and nobody else was dressed as Snow White. The cafeteria was so packed it was like looking for a needle in a haystack, literally. If she was still here, I bet I knew where she and Staci would be, the cakewalk. I made my way towards the cakewalk and there were about ten people walking the circle. I checked the line and then double-checked to be sure, but there was still no sign of my sister. Mrs. Williams was Emma's homeroom teacher and she was running the cakewalk. I don't know why I didn't notice earlier but, she liked Emma and Emma liked her. I decided I would ask her next.

"Hey, Mrs. Williams have you seen Emma? Did she return to the cakewalk?" I asked her.

"No Brendan, I haven't seen her except for when she participated in the event about an hour ago." She replied.

"Is there something wrong?" she asked me concerned.

"I just haven't been able to find her since the hayride. The last time I saw her she was with her friend Staci and I bet they took off together."

I tried to sound reassuring but deep down I was concerned for my sisters' wellbeing. I knew she was mad and the last thing I could afford to have happen was for her to tell on me again. I circled the cafeteria just to be sure. I checked all the lines then double-checked, but there was no sign of her. My next thought was to go to Staci's house and see if she followed her home. I quickly left the school hoping I was right.

Before I decided to go to Staci's, there was one other place I could check at the school and I don't know why I didn't think of it sooner. The playground. They both liked to go and play on the swings. I rushed out back to take a glance and it turned up empty. One of the swings was swaying back and forth by itself as if a ghost was having its turn on it while no one was around. The playground did look a bit creepy in the dark. I turned my back and decided to leave.

Staci's house wasn't too far from ours. It would take about twenty minutes to get to her house once I started walking. Instead of walking, I decided to run, and I liked running anyway. I passed the tractor that was used for the hayride and the owner of it hollered at me. "Hey, kid! Come here I need to speak with you about trying to scare kids." I didn't stop. I just ignored him and kept going about my way. He yelled something different at me this time, but I couldn't make it out. I was already far away.

I crossed the street going back towards home. The roads were busy with cars pulling up to houses dropping their kids off to trick-or-treat. All this traffic was slowing me down. I was dodging cars left and right. One driver honked at me and yelled. "Hey you dumb kid, get out of the road before you get hit!"

I didn't listen to him. He was right, I would get hit if I wasn't paying attention. That's why I kept my eyes forward so I could see the vehicles heading my direction. Great Halloween 2017. I'm spending it searching for my sister instead of bag snatching with my friend Derek like we had been planning all week. I'm not doing this next year.

I had three more blocks to cross and the temptation of grabbing a kid's bag had entered my mind. I know I shouldn't, but I had to at least get one since I was going through all this trouble. I really didn't want to pick on a girl but, she seemed like the best target. I didn't have time to be picky. She was dressed as what I assumed to be a fairy. Her hair was dyed purple with sparkles all in it. Her outfit was white with glitter. In her hand was a wand of some sort with a star at the end. On her back, she wore bright purple wings.

Her bag was almost full, and she had her older sister with her. I knew her sister. It was Maggie Reynolds. Maggie Reynolds was the school's biggest comic nerd. I guess that's not a bad thing since there's a lot of comic book movies coming out these days. From what I could tell, she was dressed as the Black Widow from the Avengers. I crouched behind a bush and waited patiently. I pulled down my mask and put my hood over my head. This was going to be too easy I thought. I waited for what seemed like forever, in actuality was only a matter of seconds. When they got close to my bush, I jumped out quickly, knocking Maggie on her back. The little girl's scream pierced the air around us.

"I'll be taking that!" I yelled at her.

I grabbed her bag of candy out of her hand and ran, hurrying down the street to make my getaway. That's when I felt something hard hit me in the chest. My breath escaped me as I hit the ground. When I looked up, I noticed a large man with a shaved head and a big beard scowling down at me and he was furious.

"I'll be taking that you little jerk." He said angrily.

He grabbed the bag of candy out of my hand and gave it back to the little girl I had snatched it from. Her tears were drying up from her eyes. I could tell Maggie was still shaken by the incident.

"Good job dad you got him!" Maggie said with excitement.

Her dad?! I thought, are you serious? When they weren't paying attention, I got up and started running. The big man tried to chase me down, but I got away. There was a blue van parked in front of the sidewalk. I slid right across it as you see in the movies, even with a perfect landing. I turned and looked behind me. I had left the man behind; no way was he going to catch me now. I was a little disgruntled that my victory was foiled, but glad I didn't have to stick around for the rest of it. My chest was still hurting. It was throbbing in pain from where the big man hit me. I shook it off and pressed on. Staci's house was just another block and I was sure that's where Emma was, and we could go home and be in bed before mom made it back.

I made it to Staci's house, finally, after nearly being clipped by a car. I stood looking up at the two-story Victorian-style mansion with its castle looking tops. A shutter was blowing in the wind, knocking against the side of the house. There were a few lights on. I've always thought this house looked creepy, especially at night when the two upstairs bedroom lights were on. They always looked like they were staring at you. I made my way into the front yard and listened as an owl was calling overhead. The wooden steps creaked as I stepped onto them. The wood was worn. They would need replacing soon.

The porch light was still on and I could hear a T.V. playing in the background. Good, someone was still awake. I took in a deep breath and gave the door three knocks. Knock! Knock! Knock! I waited patiently for someone to answer. After about two, maybe three minutes, I heard someone coming down the stairwell. The door opened slowly, and I could see Staci standing behind the entryway. "What do you want Brendan?" she snapped at me.

"Staci, I'm just looking for Emma. She took off shortly after you did. I checked the school twice and the playground where you and she usually hang out at and she's not there. Did she come here?" I asked nicely.

She looked at me confused as if she couldn't tell if I was lying or being sincere.

"Brendan, seriously? Are you really telling me that you can't find your sister?"

"Staci, I'm serious. Look, if she's here just go get her and tell her to come on. I'm out of breath from the run here and I was almost hit by a car. I just want to get home before our mom beats us there and gets worried. OK?"

Staci crossed her arms, but I could tell by her facial expression she was concerned. "Let me go get my phone and we'll call your house and see if she picks up because I'm going to tell you the truth. She's not here Brendan. I haven't seen her since the hayride."

Staci closed the door behind her, and I could hear her running across their hard wooden floor. About a minute later, she returned with a cell phone in her hand. "It's ringing." She said. We both listened as the phone to our house rang five times and we had to listen to our mom's silly answering machine message. Staci looked at me shaking her head.

"Try again Staci," I told her.

She hit redial, and we both listened anxiously waiting for Emma to pick up. There was no answer again, just the stupid voicemail on the other end of the line.

"Brendan do you want me to get dressed and help you," Staci asked.

"No, I'm sure she's at the house. My mom keeps the door locked. If Emma doesn't know where the key is then she can't get inside and I'm not entirely sure she does know. So, she could be sitting on the porch waiting for me." That's what I was hoping for anyway.

"Ok, well, I hope you find her and call me when you do."

I nodded my head and watched as Staci closed the door. I hoped I was right, and she was sitting on the front porch waiting for me to arrive. I started running again. My home was one block over. It would take no time for me to get there. I was irritated. The scythe I made was wearing my shoulder out as I ran holding it. I made my way down the block going to my home and I swore I saw her on the porch at the last house on the left. It was her! I couldn't mistake her. She was in her Snow-White costume feeling up her bag full of candy.

"Emma!" I called out.

Emma turned my direction and she smiled at me. I walked up on the sidewalk where she met me. "I've been looking for you everywhere Emma! Where have you been?" I asked her.

"I've been trick-or-treating. It's Halloween Brendan, what did you think I would be doing?"

"Emma, I looked for you back at the school and then I went to Staci's home and asked Staci if you were there." I answered.

"Emma I was worried. Even if you're mad at me for a prank, you shouldn't go off on your own. Somebody could have grabbed you or much worse," I scolded.

"Look, I don't want to fight tonight. I'll let you finish trick-or-treating and we'll go home, pop some popcorn and watch dumb scary movies that we can laugh at." I said.

"Ok, Brendan I just want to get the next block my bag is half full."

I nodded my head, and we made the loop. Emma grabbed my

hand. I could tell she was happy I said yes. We came up to the first house. The porch light was on and there were some kids turning to leave after they got off the porch. "Go ahead Emma, it's fine." I watched her as she ran up the steps and knocked on the door. An elderly woman wearing a flannel nightgown and big round rim glasses answered. Her hair was short and grey.

"On my, well look at you! Would you care if I took a picture of you? Snow White was my favorite fairy tale and you, little lady, look the part." The old woman asked Emma.

"I don't mind, go ahead," Emma responded with delight.

A few seconds later, the elderly woman returned with her digital camera. Emma posed for her and she took a couple of pictures. The woman gave her a few pieces of candy and Emma came trotting back, her face gleaming.

"See Brendan, it pays to be nice to people." She threw a Reese's peanut butter cup at me, which is my favorite. I tore the package open, revealing the two cups, and devoured them in a matter of seconds. "Thanks, brat those were great. I needed that." Now I just wished I had a soda to wash it down. I let Emma trick or treat another house and then she met up with some of her friends.

"Hey, Brendan can I tag along with my friends?" she asked me.

"I don't care, sis, go ahead."

I watched as her friends ran from house to house. They were excited as they filled up their bags and so were the homeowners. We finally reached the last house. It was an old, two-story red brick house with green shutters and square windows. The front light was on. Emma was the first to ring the doorbell. They waited patiently and the door opened.

The elderly man handed out a hand full of candy to all five of the kids while he chuckled, nearly losing his smoke pipe. You could tell he was glad to see the kids. We really did live in a nice neighborhood. Emma and her friends started to cross to the next house over. You've got to be kidding me. Are they really going to go to another house? I was annoyed, tired, and bummed out. I was ready to go home, but I agreed I would be a good big brother and take my sister out, and the thought of her telling on me didn't settle well with me.

I watched as she and her few remaining friends the cowboy and the witch made their way happily onto the front porch of the next home. I listened as they knocked and were welcomed by our football coach. It was Coach Stevenson. Coach Stevenson is ok. He's kind of big, like a pro-wrestler, always drinking protein shakes and working out after school. He encourages the football team to do the same. He's not a bad guy. I like him. He looked in my direction and waved when he and his pregnant wife finished giving candy to Emma and her entourage.

Emma looked both directions, ready to make her way back towards me so we could finally leave, and that's when I heard it. The loud tires squealing, trying to come to a halt, and I saw the look of terror on Emma's face as she screamed in horror.

CHAPTER 3

When I turned, all I could see was headlights. I grabbed Emma quickly and moved her out of the way of the oncoming vehicle. We both hit the pavement. I landed with a hard thud and Emma rolled into some bushes. Whoever was driving the orange Camaro didn't even stop to see if we were ok. I picked myself up and grabbed Emma.

"Are you ok sis?" I asked her.

"I'm okay, just a little shaken up. Thank you for pushing me out of the way Brendan."

"You're welcome brat. Come on, let's go so you can finish trick or treating."

I noticed she was limping, so I walked to her right side, so she was on the sidewalk and I was the one closer to the traffic in case the Camaro came speeding back. I watched as leaves skidded across the sidewalk carried by the wind. A few kids rushed past us eager to get to the next house.

Emma rushed across the next house's yard eager to knock on their door. I heard two knocks then a younger woman dressed as a witch answered. I heard Emma call out "Trick or Treat." Emma opened her bag and the woman gave her a couple of pieces of candy, what kind I couldn't tell. I heard the door slam shut and watched as Emma came running back towards my direction.

"Brendan look, it's your favorite," she called out. I looked up and in Emma's hand was a Reese's peanut butter cup.

She was right it really was my favorite. I opened the package and handed one to Emma since she had thought of me. We walked past the last house. There was no light on indicating they were participating in Trick or Treating.

"Time to go, Emma," I said to her.

We walked towards the direction of our home and came up to the cemetery.

"Hey, Emma you wanna walk through the graveyard?" I asked her excitedly.

"No, Brendan, I don't. I don't feel like hanging out where the dead rest."

"Scared much, are you?" I picked at her.

"No, I just don't like graveyards. They creep me out."

"Come on brat, it'll be fun! We'll just stay for a few minutes and then we'll go home and watch a movie until mom gets home."

Emma just took a deep breath, annoyed that I was bugging her to go with me to the cemetery. "Ok, I'll go for a couple of minutes."

We made our way to the entrance and climbed the iron gate. I should've thought to bring a flashlight, it was dark and creepy. At that moment, I slipped and started to fall. I hit hard on the cold, unforgiving ground. I had fallen into a freshly dug grave that at the present moment seemed made for me. I stood up, trying to catch my breath. The fall had knocked the wind out of me. I brushed myself off and heard Emma exclaim, "Brendan are you ok? You hurt?"

"I'm fine Emma. I just got the wind knocked out of me."

I took a deep breath and crawled out of the freshly dug grave. It was eerie as if death had touched me in his true fashion. I looked at Emma and her face wore an expression of concern.

"You sure you're ok?" she asked

"Seriously, I'm fine, although for a second, I thought I was maggot meat." I laughed.

"Ewww! That's so gross."

"What? It's true! When you die that's what happens." I teased. I watched as her face turned green with disgust.

"Your body decomposes and becomes infested with all kinds of creepy crawlies. Ok brat, I'll stop! I can tell it's making you nauseous."

"Brendan, can we please talk about something else?"

"Like what?" I asked.

"Anything but this." She replied.

"Ok, take a seat and listen to this story."

Emma sat on a concrete bench and waited for me to speak. "You remember this past summer when dad sent me to work on the Bailey Farm? He hoped that I would learn my lesson and stay out of trouble by keeping me occupied at the farm."

"One night we had a sleepover down by their fishing pond and old man Bailey told us a ghost story. It was about the goat man. He said his land was cursed by a man who was cruel to people. The man had no name and was a goat herder. Nobody knew his name, and nobody bothered him because he was so mean to others. The only thing he cared about was his goats."

"One day he was out by the pond. One of his goats was acting out. He tried whipping it with a stick. The goat cried out in pain and defied his master still. All the other goats were paying attention. They attacked their owner for his cruelty. A few days later, the authorities were dispatched to do a welfare check on the man. They found him dead at the pond. That's not the worst, though. The goats had begun to eat him. Old man Bailey says goat-man haunts the woods by his house by the pond where he died. He claims to have seen him once or twice in his life, but it's all just an old folk-tale. Nobody knows if it's true or not. Some of the other boys and I tried to find some evidence of his existence, but nothing ever turned up. Until one day when we were bailing hay."

"Nobody believed me, but I thought I saw him lurking out by the pasture. He was big, covered in matted hair with the head of a ram. I told Mr. Bailey I thought I saw the goat man. He told me it was all in my head, it was just a ghost story. I didn't argue. No one would believe me, but I'm telling you he's real."

Emma's eyes were wide with fright. My little ghost story terrified her. I was about to tell her more when I heard someone humming in the distance. I looked over my shoulder. I saw Paul, a nerdy kid in school that was always an easy target for me to pick on.

"Emma don't say anything, hide behind a tree. I'm about to play a prank on Paul," I whispered to her.

Emma didn't say anything. She scurried behind a tree close by as Paul was getting closer. I ducked back into the open grave I'd fallen into minutes ago and waited. I heard Paul coming closer.

"Hey, Paul, you wanna play?" I called out in a scary voice. I heard him stop in his steps.

"Who...who's there?" he answered nervously. I was smiling underneath my mask. He was terrified I could tell.

"In here Paul. I'm in here! Won't you come take a look?" I called back.

I heard him kneel then he peered over into the hole where I was waiting for him. I grabbed him by his arm and pulled him in with me. He started screaming. "Help me! Help me! Please, someone!" He turned and looked at me in my costume.

"Hello Paul, I'm the Reaper and your time has come. It's time for you to depart this world. I even took the liberty of digging a grave for you."

His face was full of terror. Paul whimpered in a corner, not even willing to try to make a run for it. I pulled my mask off and started to laugh uncontrollably at him.

"You screamed like a little girl Paul! I'm gonna tell everyone at school on Monday how you cried like a baby."

Paul stood up, humiliated and embarrassed. He climbed out of the grave. I started to follow when I felt a sharp pain hit my fingers. Paul had stomped on top of my hand, and I lost my grip from the pain that shot through my fingers and I fell back into the hole. I was angry. When I finally climbed out of the grave, Paul was long gone, and I could hear Emma laughing her head off at me.

"You can't be mad at him for getting you back. You deserved it and you know it," she laughed hysterically.

"Nobody asked you." I grumbled.

Paul would get his for this. I would make sure of it. I had to give him credit though. He got me when I wasn't looking. My thumb was throbbing. It felt broken and it hurt to wiggle it. I just shut the pain out of my mind.

"Come on Emma, let's go home before mom gets there and wonders where we're at."

We walked out of the cemetery. The clouds covered the moon and the stars were bright. I stared up at Orion, the hunter, my favorite constellation. I guess I like Orion because he was big and strong. Everything I hoped to be. We made our way back towards our house. We had a ten-minute walk ahead of us.
I noticed Emma wasn't limping anymore. That was a sign of relief. I made sure to keep a sharp eye on the road and noticed the old Broadway Theater. I grabbed Emma by the shoulder.

"Hey look," I said.

Emma turned and looked with me.

"Brendan, how did we get here? We should be almost home, not clear across town."

That was my thought. It didn't make any sense. I was sure we went the right way. We were only ten minutes from the house or so I thought.

"Emma it doesn't make sense. I know we went the right direction." I said trying to keep her calm. I watched as an old streetlight flickered in the distance then finally went out.

"Come on Emma it's not too late, let's go check it out." She sighed loudly.

"Emma come on, I wanna see it. Don't you remember mom telling us? She won beauty pageants here when she was younger. It would be cool to see."

I didn't care about not being home on time. I've wanted to explore the old theater ever since I could remember, and now I finally had the chance. Emma followed my lead across the street, and we stared up at the old brick building that was now condemned.

I opened the door and we crept inside slowly. There were cobwebs everywhere and the building smelled like my locker room laundry after practice. The old concession stand was covered in years old dust. One of the curtains lay across the floor molding in water from a leak that came through the ceiling. In a weird way, I liked the place. My curiosity almost felt satisfied. I turned and looked over at Emma. "Isn't this place great?" I asked her.

"Only you could think this place was awesome. Brendan, we need to go. We could get hurt in here if we're not careful and no one would know about it but us."

"You need to stop worrying. We'll be fine. Let's check out the front where the stage is."

I opened the big wooden door to the entryway. The old theater was amazing. Some of the seats were still intact, while others laid over and some had rips in the cushions. The crystal chandelier still hung from the ceiling. I'm surprised no one had taken it by now. There were maybe two hundred seats. The red carpet was loose and ripped.

"Hey, brat, let's get on the stage."

"Brendan the wood may not hold you. You could fall through and break your leg."

I didn't listen as I made my way up the stairs. They didn't look trustworthy. I placed my right foot down on the first one. It creaked but it held my weight. I made it to the top of the stage. I couldn't imagine what it must have felt like to be an actor and put on a show in front of everyone. I would've been too nervous. I heard Emma coming up the steps behind me. I watched as she made her way towards me.

"Emma you can't tell me this isn't cool," I said.

"You're right! It's too cool," she exclaimed.

I watched as she started skipping across the platform. I was happy to see her having a good time again. She made a few more laps, then she stopped and stared behind my shoulder blade. The look on her face said it all. I watched as tears welled up in her eyes. She glanced at me for a second and then pointed behind me. I took a deep breath and turned slowly, and for the first time in a long time I felt scared.

CHAPTER 4

I stared up at a being that stood almost twelve feet tall. It wore a red cloak and its eyes were sharp and red. I watched as bat wings spread from its back. They were huge and they wrapped around its shoulders like a cape. I took a step back slowly and grabbed Emma. It pointed its long bony finger at me.

"Brendan!" it called out. Its voice boomed like thunder.

"What are you?" I asked.

"I am the spirit of Samhain. Perhaps you've heard of me," it answered.

I thought for a moment. I've heard the name, but I couldn't place it.

"I'm not sure, so maybe you can tell me again who you are?" I answered.

The large being stared hard at me angrily and I watched his wings spread again from his back. "I'm the spirit of Halloween. I'm the reason you have Halloween," his voice boomed.

"Please! Please! don't hurt us," Emma asked of him. I watched as she started to cry. I tried to put her at ease, but it didn't work. Samhain just kept his eyes on us. I tried to look at his face, but the shadow of his hood kept it covered. He loomed closer to us. I stood my ground, prepared for whatever might happen next.

"You two need to sit and listen and I will explain my appearance here tonight. I'm going to tell you about who I am and why I've chosen you two tonight." I swallowed hard. Emma was shaking uncontrollably. I placed my hand on her shoulder, trying to ease her nerves. It didn't work.

"I said sit down!" Samhain's voice boomed. I decided to do what he said since I didn't have another plan and I didn't think we could escape from him.

"Now that I finally have you two mortals' attention, I will continue. I've already told you who I am, but I haven't explained as to what I am. I'm the spirit of Halloween, as I told you earlier. You mortals worshiped me generations ago. Mortals would dress in masks pretending to be spirits so my spirits couldn't possess you. You wore masks as you do now to try to ward them off. The mortals' fear of me is what made me strong."

"Then somehow it became a tradition for you young ones to wear costumes and receive candy for it and you call it Halloween when it was once called All Hallows Eve. Many once feared me. A few mortals worshiped me like a god and left me offerings of food and drink. My name wasn't spoken aloud out of fear of my appearing at the slightest mention of my name. People were punished severely.

"The mortals were scared to come out at night. You would carry salt to try to ward off the spirits of the forgotten and me. Now you've forgotten about me completely. You carve pumpkins and decorate your yards with witches and ghosts. Well, I decided it's time to do something about that, and it starts with you two." I looked around the theater and saw that the spirits of the dead surrounded us.

"So, let me get this straight, you're the almighty and powerful Samhain that everyone used to fear and now because you've been forgotten, you want to pick on two kids. That's how you plan on making your return as the almighty scary one? By the way, I've never even heard of you." I smirked.

"Hey, Emma, look it's Samhain master of Halloween all forgotten about!" I joked. Emma began to laugh with me. Samhain didn't see the humor in my response and lunged for us bellowing ominously.

"Emma Run!" I screamed. We made a dash for the stairs past Samhain and ran towards the exit door. Some spirits that had the exit door blocked stopped us. I swung my scythe at them. I watched as it went through them like thin air, they were ghosts after all. There was nothing I could do to protect us.

"Brendan, what do we do?" Emma asked me terrified.

I tried to push through the two spirits. The one who looked like a woman grabbed me by the shoulder and pushed me down to the floor hard. I stood up determined to get past them. I tried again but it didn't work. I ended up on my back again.

"Bring them to me!" I heard Samhain command.

Ghostly hands were all over Emma and me. The spirits surrounded us and lifted us up off our feet and above their heads. I tried to scramble away but I couldn't free myself from their grip. I looked up as they dropped us back on the hard, wooden floor of the stage in front of Samhain. I was truly terrified and had never felt more helpless than I did right then as they threw us down hard at his feet.

Laughter plagued our ears. Our attempt to escape seemed futile. I had to wait for another opportunity to present itself then I would try again. "So, you thought you could escape, did you?"

"I'll give you credit. You tried, but at least you made an attempt. Usually most kids they freeze, because their terrified and unsure of what to do next. "

"What do you want from us?" I asked.

The room grew still. All the spirits stopped laughing and even

Samhain paused.

"What do I want Brendan you ask? I want you to fear me like you have made all those other children fear you in the past. I've been watching you carefully Brendan, and I must say I'm happy with my choice. I think you will prove quite the opponent tonight."

I was confused. I'm going to be his opponent. What did he mean by that? "Care to elaborate on that Mr. Halloween?"

Samhain's voice boomed with frustration "It means, Brendan, that tonight you're going to undergo a couple of tests if you and your little sister wish to make it home tonight."

"You, Brendan, will face your fears. If you can conquer two of your greatest fears, then finally you will face me. Every year on Halloween I find a child and make them face their fears."

"When they fail--and they all do--I grow even stronger because of it. I would also like to mention that when they fail, they become one of my spirits doomed to walk this earth and serve me. I just want you to know what's at stake here for you and your sister so there's no confusion about what's going on."

Inside I was laughing. I don't have any fears. Everyone fears me, so this should be easy. "Hey, Samhain, there's just one problem with that. I don't have any fears. There's nothing you can use against me!" I shouted mockingly.

"You're wrong Brendan. You just think there's nothing that scares you. Deep down I know that isn't true, and so do you. It will prove interesting to see how well you do with all that arrogance you carry inside of you."

"Brendan stop being so macho! He's serious and scary can't you tell!" Emma shouted at me.

"Ok Samhain, I'll entertain you, and I'll beat you! Bring everything you can, cause you're going to need it. I told you I don't fear anything. Everyone fears me with good reason. They know I'm the bully and I'll even prove it to you, oh Great Spirit of Halloween who has to pick on kids to feel good about himself." I scoffed.

"Brendan I was right in choosing you. Your confidence is entertaining, but it will prove useless when you see what terrible things lie ahead for you. I am the master of fear; I represent all the things you're afraid of. Good luck!"

"Well, why are we still talking? Let's do this so I can beat you."

That was when I fell asleep. All I remember was my body going limp as I collapsed.

CHAPTER 5

I awoke in my bed confused and puzzled by what just happened. Was it all just a bad dream I'd had? I threw my covers off and jumped out of my bed. That's weird...I was still in my reaper costume. I looked out the window. The moon was still full, and the stars were shining. Ok, I thought. I decided to check around the house and see where Emma and my mother were. I grabbed my scythe that lay in my bed, opened my bedroom door, and proceeded to Emma's room.

I took a deep breath as I walked alone in the darkness to Emma's room. I was sure she was asleep, but in the back of my mind, I had the worst feeling of foreboding. This was the first time I'd not felt safe in my own home. I turned Emma's doorknob slowly and entered her room.

I saw the outline of someone lying in bed. I had to be sure it was her. I reached for the light switch to turn on her bedroom light. When the light came on it was just one of her stuffed animals laying in her spot. I opened her closet door to check and found nothing...just her clothes and the stuffed animals she had collected over the years. I peeked in her bathroom. It was empty too. I could find no sign that Emma had been in her room.

I turned her light off and closed the door. Maybe they're down in the living room asleep. I made my way towards the stairwell and descended the stairs. The stairs creaked under my feet. I made my way towards the living room and turned on the light switch. No one was there. Where are they? I thought to myself. It's got to be a prank. They're paying me back for all the jokes I've pulled on them in the past.

I searched the kitchen for signs they were here, like dirty dishes or maybe the smell of popcorn. Nothing. The dishes were in place and nothing looked out of place or disturbed. The house was too neat. I checked my parent's room with no luck. No one was home. I opened the screen door that led outside to our back porch. My father's grill was in its place. The night air was cool. I heard our porch swing swaying in the slight breeze, the chain squeaked as it swung back and forth.

"Mom! Dad! Emma! Where are you?" I called out. I waited for a response and heard nothing.

I walked back inside my home frustrated. This suddenly didn't feel like a prank anymore. "Come on you guys jokes over," I yelled, angry with either them or the situation, I wasn't sure. Still, nothing.

I roamed through the house one more time to double-check, and I was still right. There was no one home. I checked the refrigerator for a note and found nothing. Unsure of what to do next, I grabbed my skateboard by the front door and walked back outside towards our front lawn. The screen door slammed behind me with a hard thud.

It took me a minute to realize that none of the houses on my street were decorated with the Halloween decorations they'd had earlier tonight. Now I knew for sure something was truly wrong. All the streetlights were out, no porch lights, no sign of life at all. I grabbed my skateboard and hit the pavement.

Skateboarding has always been a passion of mine, an escape. Tony Hawk was who inspired me to skate.
I skated down the street not sure what I was looking for other than signs of life or someone I could talk to. The street looked like nothing more than a ghost town with all the lights out. The only

sound was that of the wind howling. I went door to door to every house and knocked. I got no answer, and all the doors were locked. I felt hopeless and alone.

I remembered suddenly what Samhain had told me. He said I would face my fears. Fears I didn't know I had. Is being alone one of them? Did he know something about me that I didn't know about myself? The theater was where we had been just before I passed out. I decided to go check it out. Maybe what happened there was just a joke or all in my head.

I hopped on my board and started to skate down the block. It would only take maybe ten to fifteen minutes to get there from my street. I used my right foot to pick up speed and I leaned my body weight forward and gripped my scythe in my left hand. I had to get there quickly.

The streets were clear and dark, and all the streetlights were black. I stepped onto the curb by the theater, took a deep breath and went inside. In the lobby, I looked for a light switch and flicked it on. The light flickered. I kept telling myself that I had to be brave. I steeled myself, opened up the door and walked into the theater. To my surprise, it was dark and empty. There was no sign of Samhain or my family. Now what? I wondered. I left the theater without hesitation.

I skated up to Staci's house and came to a stop in front of the porch. The lights were out just like everywhere else I had been. I wondered if Emma had come back here to stay the night and if Mom had left with Dad. I walked up the steps leading to the front door and rang the doorbell. I waited for about a minute, which felt like an hour. There was no answer. I tried again and waited patiently. There was still no answer. I didn't want to look like a creeper, but I peeked through the windows and saw nothing but total darkness. Where could everyone be? My only other thought now was that the town was abandoned and somehow, I'm still here.

The more I thought about it, the more it felt true. Samhain was playing a trick on me and it was my turn to figure it out. Ok, Samhain you want to play? Let's play! I walked back down the steps and crossed through Staci's front lawn. I just wanted to see someone, anyone, it didn't matter who at this point.

"What do you want Samhain? Huh, what do you want from me?" I screamed. "You think you can scare me? I'm right here waiting for you!" There was no response, just silence. All I could hear was the wind howling.

"Samhain, you're a coward! Why don't you come out?" I screamed again. The situation reminded me of when I was eight years old. My mom and dad had taken me to a theme park that summer to ride the rides. I couldn't get on the big boom coaster because I didn't meet the height requirements. I was so upset about it. It didn't matter what the other rides were, I wanted to be a big boy and ride the big boy ride.

That was when I got lost in the park. I looked for what felt like hours for my parents. There were people everywhere. You could smell the cotton candy and freshly popped popcorn. I was so scared because this was the first time, I had gotten lost. I remember finding a worker and approaching them, my eyes filled with tears. I told him I had gotten lost and couldn't find my parents. The man was very nice to me. He led me to the front and gave me a free bag of popcorn while he looked for my parents.

It was about an hour later that they showed up with a security officer looking for me. My mother had been crying. She was so upset and relieved to see me all at the same time, and so was my father. Emma was a lot smaller than I was back then, and much less annoying.

I took a deep breath and skated back to the house. It was the only place I felt safe. I made it to the house in about five minutes. It still looked empty. Truthfully, I didn't want to go back inside. I was too afraid to face the disappointment that the house would still be as empty as the rest of the neighborhood.

I sat down on top of my skateboard with my fingers intertwined, pondering for a few minutes what my next move would be. That's when I heard a deep growl coming from behind me. I stood up and looked behind me. At first, I didn't see anything except the creatures menacing red eyes peering at me from within the shadows of my front porch. I watched, shaking at its large shadow cast in the light of the moon. Whatever it was, it was huge and muscular. Its yellow teeth were razor-sharp, and horns protruded out the top of its head.

I thought for a moment the dog looked familiar. I remembered now... It's Buster! I swallowed hard. This giant size bulldog is the reason why I have a scar down the left side of my leg. He bit me when I was eight as I was walking down the road. I remember how bad I bled. My parents were so furious at my neighbors. Mr. Harper was a mean old man who used to live next door to us. His dog was just as mean as he was. I remember my dad called the police. He wanted the dog put down. He told them the dog was too aggressive. My father and Mr. Harper got into a fight about it on the front lawn. My dad got the best of Mr. Harper that day, and the police agreed the dog had to be put to sleep. The dogcatcher was called, and they took possession of Buster. A week later, the dog was euthanized, and Mr. Harper moved away.

Now here before me, Buster lives, and he's bigger. So are his teeth. One of my worst fears I had forgotten about had come back to life and I was about to be his next chew toy. I could see it now Buster gets his revenge. Buster made his way slowly down the porch steps. He growled again, but this time was more menacing than the last. I had to think, and quickly. I hoped I could outrun him. I backed away slowly into the street, not taking my eyes off Buster. Buster leapt at me, and I swung my skateboard like a baseball bat hitting him at the top of his head. The force of his weight still knocked me down. I rolled on the pavement across the street.

I grabbed my skateboard and started to skate down the street. I heard Buster close behind me. All I could think about was that I had to get away and quick. I turned and looked. He was gaining on me.

All I could hear behind me was Buster gnashing his sharp teeth as he looked forward to biting me with them. I looked behind me again and saw that Buster was still gaining on me. I had to come up with something. I needed a place to hide and get away quickly. I needed to slow Buster down. But how? I felt his teeth tear a piece of cloth from my reaper costume. I swung my scythe as hard as I could at him with the broom handle end. When the broom handle hit the side of his head, it sounded hollow. He yelped in pain and stopped. Good, I slowed him down. A small gash appeared where the blow had landed, and a trickle of blood flowed down the side of his mane. "Yes!" I screamed aloud. I didn't have time to celebrate my short victory. I wanted to put as much distance between the two of us as I could.

I turned to look one more time. Buster let out a loud, menacing howl and started towards my direction again. I watched for a brief second as the overgrown dog charged through a wooden fence breaking one of the posts in half. It didn't hurt Buster now I realized. It only made him mad. Now, I was truly scared of what he might do to me if he caught me.

My victory was short-lived. I should go to the school where I could surely hide from him until I came up with an idea of how to stop the overgrown mutt. I pressed on down the street. I didn't bother to look behind me anymore. Instead, I leaned into my board, making my way downhill. I knew I could gain speed and get ahead of him.

The school was only a half-mile from where I was. I leaned in more on my board, almost losing my balance as I rounded the curve. I could hear Buster gaining on me. I needed a distraction. I wasn't going to make it unless I slowed him down again. I looked at my surroundings and saw a streetlight by a boat hitched to a trailer. I had an idea. I just hoped it worked.

I took my scythe and stretched it out by the streetlight, hooking the blade onto it. It swung me around in a circle so fast the front end of my board came off the ground. Buster leapt at me again and missed. I was right. He crashed headfirst into the boat, almost knocking it off the ground. He left a good size dent in the side of it. Someone was going to be upset.

The momentum from me swinging myself around the pole gave me a good head start again. I didn't want to wait around to see if he got up. If I won, I'm sure Samhain would show how upset he was. I had to beat Buster for Emma. I neared the corner. I turned and didn't see Buster anywhere. I still didn't plan to stick around and wait to be his supper. I could see the school in the distance. I was almost there. I sighed with relief. I remembered my teacher Mrs. Webb had a habit of leaving her classroom window unlocked. I just had to get to her window, and I could crawl in. I already knew the back entrance of the school and the two front entrances would be locked. I stopped in front of the school and took a couple of deep breaths. I hadn't realized how tired I was.

My underclothes were soaked in sweat. I guess it didn't help that I was wearing a thick costume. My throat was dry. I was thirsty and I needed to quench it. I picked up my board and made my way around back to the playground where my school held recess. I was still gasping for wind and my legs felt cramped up. I saw Mrs. Webb's window. A smile broadened my face. Now, how to get up there? I had an idea. I took the broom handle of my scythe and broke out the window.

I covered my face with my skull mask as the glass fell from the window. Lucky me, I wasn't even nicked by any of the shards. I took my scythe and used it as a grappling hook to lift me up. I pulled myself up and wrapped my left hand in cloth to wipe away the glass so I wouldn't cut myself. The window was safe for me to crawl through.

I pulled myself through the window. All of a sudden, I felt a hard tug on the bottom of my right foot and was almost pulled out of the window. It was Buster. He had caught up with me. This dog was tough. His gash was opened up even more. I saw the thick red blood pouring down the side of his face. He pulled again and this time he almost pulled me down. I had to think fast. There was a piece of glass I had missed in the corner of the window. I grabbed it out of instinct. I only had one shot at the big dog.

Buster was getting ready to have me as his chew toy. I swung the glass cutting open his nose. He yelped in pain, letting go of my shoelace. I crawled through the window as quickly as I could. I got away. Buster was still whimpering in pain from the wound I had just given him. I remembered Mrs. Webb liked cricket. She had a cricket stick by her desk. That would work if the dog managed to get inside. I grabbed the large stick and twisted the doorknob leading to the main hallway of the school. I skated towards the front entrance. My heart sank as I reached the entrance doors.

The door was locked from the inside with a padlock and chain. I had forgotten that our school locked the entrance doors this way. I was done for I thought. I heard a loud crash come from the back of the school, and then another. I knew what it was Buster was trying to break the door down. I took the cricket stick and swung hard striking the padlock. It didn't work. I heard another crash.

This time it sounded like he was breaking through the back door. had an idea. I could wrap the chain around the stick and use it to inflict more damage to Buster's head. I couldn't run anymore. I had to face Buster. I quickly wrapped the chain around the stick and used the lock to hold it in place. I heard another crash. This time the back door opened. I could hear Buster's huge paws making their way through the hallway, making their way towards me. Brendan, you better know what you're doing. His footsteps echoed throughout the hallway he was close now. I could hear his loud angry barks. I could see him now. The giant mutt was moving fast, his red eyes locked on me. I tightened my grip.

I got in position for a baseball swing. I took a deep breath and let it out. It was either me or him and I would do whatever it took to make sure it wasn't going to be me. His mouth opened, ready to tear me apart. I could see the blood had stained his teeth. I took a quick sidestep and swung the stick as hard as I could. I connected. I hit him right where I'd gashed him on the side of his head earlier. There was a loud crunching sound that sounded like bones breaking. Buster collapsed to the floor. The stick, even with the chain wrapped around it, broke in two. I took a deep breath.

My heart pounding hard in my chest, I glanced towards Buster. He wasn't breathing. Then I saw all the blood. I had broken his neck. Buster was dead again for the second time.

I fell to my knees and my entire body was shaking. I did it. I defeated one of my fears. I defeated Buster. A tear escaped my eye. I reached for my scythe and my board. I saw a water fountain and knew I needed to quench my thirst. The water felt refreshing in the back of my throat. I examined Buster one more time just to make sure he was really dead. His blood now stained the hallway from the front door. I had no doubt now. I made my way back outside into the night air. As I left the school, I fell to the pavement from the shock of having fought the fight of my life.

CHAPTER 6

Have you ever had a dream where you're falling and right before you hit, you wake up? Well, after my battle with Buster this was how I woke up. As I was falling, I could see Samhain and all his minions on the stage. I awoke right before I hit the hardwood floor. I took in a deep breath and stood up quickly, trying to gather my senses along with my surroundings. My right hand was clenched tightly into a fist, and in my left hand was my scythe. I wiped the sweat from my eyes trying to clear my vision and I saw Samhain again. He was holding Emma. I was back.

"You did well, Brendan, you didn't disappoint. You put on a good show. I'm afraid I underestimated you. You have wit and courage. You're also smart on your feet. For that, I do compliment you." Samhain spoke up.

"It will not be enough, I'm afraid. Your next challenge is going to be more difficult. Most don't make it past the second challenge. It proves difficult for them because their fears are too challenging, and they just give up."

"You could face me yourself you overgrown bat!" I shouted.

All of Samhain's spirits stopped laughing. The room grew quiet. I waited for his response.

"You little childish fool! I'm Samhain, the true spirit of everything that is Halloween. You foolishly challenge me. I take it as a compliment. I will say this to you, Brendan, you are brave but, stupid very stupid." Samhain shouted.

"I tell you what, Brendan. If you make it through this test, you will have your wish. You can face, me, but I hope you're prepared to meet your end because I've never been defeated at my own game.

"I look forward to it!" I scoffed at him. "Samhain, I want you to know something and to understand me clearly. I'm not afraid of you."

"Brendan shut up; you're only making it worse! Don't let your ego distract you!" Emma called to me.

I turned and looked in her direction. She was still being held captive by Samhain's spirits. She was right, to a point. I couldn't let my ego get in the way, but my plan was to frustrate Samhain so he would lose his focus on her and redirect it to me. I saw an opening when he turned his back, and I skated towards Emma. I struck one of the skeletons holding Emma captive with my scythe, knocking its bones across the stage like bowling pins.

Before I could reach her, Samhain reached out, swatting at me as if I were a fly. He slammed me backwards at least twenty feet, knocking the breath out of me. "That was very foolish of you, noble, but still foolish little boy." Samhain and his followers laughed mockingly at me. I brushed myself off and stood up again.

"Brendan, I do hope you survive this next time, I really do. It's been a hundred years since a kid has tested me. So, we'll see if you're worthy or not. It would be a great pleasure for me to defeat you so I can go on living and build my army of followers."

Suddenly, my vision began to blur, and I felt dizzy. I could hear Emma calling my name, but her voice sounded miles away. The last thing I remember was my head crashing violently onto the hardwood floor of the old stage.

I came to suddenly, visibly shaken. My body was trembling like it was in shock. I looked around and discovered I was l standing on the pavement in front of my home again. This time, it looked different. Ash was falling from the orange-red sky. What happened here? I asked myself. A terrible stench filled my nose. Whatever the smell was, it was gross. It smelled like something had been rotting for a long time. It was worse than the smell of mildew or a cow pasture. The stink was ten times worse than the whiff you get while driving past a cow pasture with your window down. I felt sick to my stomach. If my stomach had been full, I think I would've yelled at my shoes if you know what I mean. The air was humid and muggy. What happened here?

"Well, here we go again Brendan," I said aloud to myself.

I was curious to see what Samhain had in store for me now. I still had my board and Scythe. Good. I dusted myself off and gathered my courage for whatever was to come next.

I took a couple of steps towards my home and realized what looked different about it. My house was older and looked decayed. The paint was peeling off the sides of the house, the window shutters were loose, and the chimney looked like somebody had blown it up. The bricks were scattered across the roof and the ground below. The roof shingles looked worn and in desperate need of replacing. The house looked like it had been abandoned for years. I looked at the other homes and they looked abandoned as well. The vehicles appeared old and faded, with the doors ripped from the hinges and their tires flat.

I decided to investigate further. I didn't have to open the door to my home it had fallen off its hinges. I stepped inside and heard the creak of the floor beneath my feet. The house reeked. Water dripped from the ceiling as the furniture smelled stale and moldy. I covered my nose.

I walked towards the kitchen. I could see food that had been set out on the table left to rot. Bacteria was growing from inside the potatoes and fruit on the table. The refrigerator was turned over facing down and brown water was flowing out of it. I didn't want to step in it, but I had to continue forward to check out the rest of the home. I made my way towards the stairs. They weren't in good shape either. The railing was broken off. I had to be careful, so I didn't fall and hurt myself. Electrical wires were dangling from the ceiling where tiles had fallen in and broken on the floor. I'm not sure what I was hoping to find, maybe a glimmer of hope that my parents were alive and well.

I felt the stair collapse as I put my weight on it. I stepped up to the top of the stairway quickly to avoid the fall. That was close. I shook my head in frustration. How many more times will I get lucky through this whole ordeal? I remembered what Samhain had said. "People don't usually make it through the second challenge." I was about to show him I'm not most people. I was determined to win this.

My house reminded me of a horror game I liked to play. It was about the apocalypse where humans went mad and turned on each other. The object of the game was to survive and save as many people as you can in the process. You had to defeat a general who had a doctor create the virus that turns everyone mad. The game was scary to play with the music that was built into it, especially at night. It gave my sister a nightmare when we were home by ourselves one night. A thunderstorm had moved in which blended in with the game perfectly. The video game was called The Rest of Us. It was a present from my mom and dad for Christmas last year when I got my PlayStation 4. The first time I remember playing it was at Derek's house. It's his fault I'm the gamer I am now.

I walked into my sister's room first. I opened the door slowly and was hit with a foul stench that took me to my knees. I'm not even sure I wanted to look inside, but I hit the light switch and the light flickered, illuminating a nest of dead birds in her room. I shut the door hard behind me.

"Mom? Dad?" I called out.

There was no response, but it was what I expected. I decided I didn't want to explore anymore, but there was the issue of getting back to the first floor since the stairs had collapsed when I was walking up them earlier. So, I continued my search of the upstairs rooms.

I walked towards my room and opened the door, uncertain of what I would find. I flicked the light switch on so I could see inside and heard a loud pop! My light bulb blew out. I treaded carefully and walked right into the spider's web. Deep down I hate spiders, especially their webs.

As I made my way further into the room, I looked up and saw that my room was full of spider webs. Webs were everywhere! Great! Just great! I had the idea to take my sheets, tie them into knots, and make a rope I could repel down to the ground I pulled the sheets from my bed and hundreds of spiders scattered everywhere. I hurried and tied the knot. I wanted out of here...I tested the knot to make sure it was secure. Holding the loose end of the sheets in my hand, I made a run for the window and jumped outside.

I was falling and felt the sheets tighten. My body swung hitting the side of the house hard, and I fell on my right side. It didn't hurt--not too much anyway. I stood up, brushing myself, checking to make sure the spiders were gone. I saw a few crawling on the ground and stomped on them with my shoes.

"I hate spiders!" I shouted.

Come on, Brendan, get it together! You're the tough guy, remember? The guy all the other kids are afraid to mess with and you're afraid of spiders. You just defeated Buster. You can deal with spiders!

I walked towards the front of the house where the wooden fence used to be. It now lay on the ground with pieces of the posts split in two. I made my way back up to the porch where I had laid my skateboard and scythe against the wall and grabbed them.

Frustration was starting to build. I was getting mad again. I just wanted this whole ordeal to be finished. I wanted to be home with my mom and dad playing my video games or hanging out with Derek, scaring Staci and my sister or making fun of other kids in school. I told myself if I ever get out of this, I would stop bullying. I mean it. I will stop.

I placed my board down on the pavement unsure of where to go and what to do. To my right, I saw what looked like a crowd of people scattered around like ants when you kick their anthill. Instead of skating, I wanted the element of surprise so I walked slowly and quietly. There were cars parked on the road. One was a 2016 Mustang and the entire front end was knocked in. Man, what a waste I thought.

I edged closer, hid behind an old GMC van, and put my head down making sure I was going without being noticed.. I still couldn't shake the smell that lingered in the air. It was horrible! I crept even closer and ducked down behind a fence. I was only a few yards away from the crowd of people standing in the street. Some of them were breaking into houses looking for something. But, what? I thought. I inched closer.

The realization hit me once I got a good look at them. They weren't people! I mean, they were, but they weren't. They were zombies and they were searching through houses, probably looking for something to eat. Well, this is just great. Now I have to fight a gang of zombies who could no doubt rip me to shreds if they wanted to. There were a bunch of them, too! Possibly twenty at the most.

"We need to keep searching. Surely there is something to eat around here."

"They can talk!" I said aloud. Oops. I didn't mean say that so loud. One of the zombies turned and looked in my direction.

"Over there! Did you hear that? There's someone here with us." It called out.

I watched closely as two stumbled my direction. I had to think fast! Where could I escape? I was still hiding behind this fence. I couldn't go right because the house next to me looked boarded up. I had to go left down the street, which meant they would notice me, and a chase would no doubt ensue. As soon as the big one with his left eye dangling out of his eye socket edged near me, I stepped out and swung my scythe hard at his head knocking it off his shoulders. I watched as his head rolled across the pavement towards the others.

The second one, which was tall and walked with a limp due to half his right foot was missing lunged at me. I took a step back and planted my left foot. I shifted my weight and threw a hard-right hand into his gut, knocking him to his knees. I kicked him hard in the face with my right foot... I watched as both his eyes rolled out of their sockets. One of the other zombies that was making its way towards me stepped on the eyes, and I heard a loud squish under its boots.

The zombie who I knocked on the ground yelled back at me, "My eyes! He knocked out my eyes! I can't see anything! I'm gonna get you human!"

"Good luck with that! One of your buddies just stepped on them and squashed them under his boots," I answered. The sound of the zombie's eyes squashing sounded like my dad when he would pass gas after eating Mexican food. My mom would get so irritated at him while Emma and I would laugh.

I knew I had to face the zombies, but first I had to come up with a plan to defeat them. I skated ahead before they caught me. There were too many of them. I could use some help right about now, Samhain said I had good instincts, which means he was worried because I'm so resourceful. Come on, Brendan, you can come up with something. I looked behind me and saw about fifteen zombies… Could I take them by myself?

I made a mad dash on my skateboard and started to skate down the block. OK, so now, I'm stuck in a world that looks post-apocalyptic and everyone is a zombie. This was another of my childhood fears. The zombies were chasing me. I looked behind me, and they were gaining on me. I was zigzagging down the street dodging cars. One slip up and I was done for.

I had to gain speed! I leaned into my board, trying to gain speed again. I came to an opening in the road and mounted the curve. There were no cars in sight. I leaned in further. I was picking up speed, going faster and faster. I turned, and one zombie leapt at me trying to grab me by my ankles. I cut the curve and took a sharp right. He barely missed me. I came to the downhill. The downhill is a sheer hill we're all scared to ride down. It's so steep, some kids from my school have broken their ankles, arms, and just about anything you can think of, it's happened.

I stopped at the edge and looked down. There were no cars in my way. I looked behind me. I saw the mob and they were coming to my direction pretty quickly. I only had maybe a minute to make a decision. I could stay and fight the mob of zombies, or I could be the first kid to descend the downhill without injury. If I stayed, I might lose the fight. If I descend the downhill, I might break a leg and lose anyway.

I made my decision. I took the hill. I placed my board back down and took a deep breath. Here goes nothing. I started my descent downhill. I didn't even bother to look behind me. I was leaning as far down as I could into my board, almost placing my weight into my right knee. I whipped past a trash can. The wind was blowing hard into my face. My eyes were starting to tear up. I was almost to the bottom then I felt my board start to shake.

"Please don't, please don't, you're almost there Brendan," I said aloud.

For a second, I thought I was going to lose my balance, but I made it through. I made it all the way down the downhill. My eyes were still tearing up from the speed I had gained. I needed a place to hide so I could collect myself. I knew a place, and I could get there quickly if I kept going. Suddenly, I struck something, and I hit the ground hard. I skidded across someone's parking lot, my body slamming hard into a wooden fence. Guess who won? The fence didn't give an inch. I looked up and saw what I had hit. I had hit a man. His body was laying on the road. His right arm was twisted. From the angle he was laying, it looked broken. I grabbed my scythe up from the ground. I don't know how, but I was lucky it landed next to me.

Man, my body hurt from that crash. That's when I heard him groan. I froze, my body tensed up, and I looked towards his direction. I watched as he slowly started to push himself up from the ground. I was right his right arm was broken. Then his head turned towards me, and I stared in shock. I couldn't believe who I was looking at. It was my father. I had hit my father coming down the downhill. "Dad, are you ok?" I asked him.

My father just looked at me confused as if he didn't even know me. "Dad, are you ok?" I asked him again. I started to walk towards him, and then I stopped and took a closer look. Half of his face was missing on the left side. My heart sank. I realized that my father was a zombie just like the ones I had just left behind on the downhill. A tear slowly escaped my eye. I looked around for my skateboard. It was behind my father who was making his way towards me.

"Son, I'm sorry! I can't help it, I'm just so hungry!" My father said to me.

"Dad, don't! I don't wanna do this." I looked and saw that the other zombies had made their way downhill and were coming in our direction. I hit my dad with a hard-left cross to the face. He stumbled backwards, landing on his back. I scrambled over him and made my way towards my board. I retrieved my board and started skated away from the advancing zombies. I could hear my father yelling at me, “Brendan! Brendan! You have to stop! We're just so hungry!”

I had no time to be emotional right now. For the first time in a long time, I just wanted to cry, and tough guys like me just didn't do that. I looked behind me and realized they were gaining on me. These zombies were fast, and they weren't slowing down, either. I needed to slow them down. But, how? I looked all around me for anything I could use that would give me a little bit of leverage. I found it. I spotted a logging chain lying atop a rusted brown tow truck from Crazy Bob's Towing. Everyone said old Bob was crazy, but my father said he was simply different and misunderstood. I think my dad was the only person who liked Crazy Bob, and he said that Bob was good at his job, too. I quickly grabbed the logging chain with my left hand and waited for the zombies to get closer.

The zombies started to surround me. I wasn't sure if my idea was foolish, or if it would even work. I waited until they edged closer. Once they got within closing distance, I started to spin on my board in a 360, swinging the chain above my head. I heard the chain whip and hit some of the zombies in the head, knocking them down to the ground. There was some still coming, So I kept swinging. I watched as head after head split open. I was dizzy for only a second. I'm not sure exactly how many zombies were trying to kill me, but I managed to defeat all of them.

I needed something else though, something that would stop them permanently. I started checking inside Crazy Bob's tow truck. There was nothing inside. I spotted a gas can on the back of the tow truck that I thought could work. I just prayed it wasn't empty. I grabbed it from the back of the vehicle. It was about half full. That could work. I scurried back to where the zombies had fallen and began pouring the gas around them. I then poured a trail of gas leading away from them as I retreated. Now I just needed something to light the gas. I found a matchbook inside the glove compartment of the tow truck.

As I made my way back to the gas trail, I noticed her in the mix of all the other zombies She was looking directly at me. My mother was now a zombie. I had forgotten for a brief moment that my dad was one, too. So, of course, my mother would be one. Samhain you're going to pay for this. Deep down I knew this wasn't real but, it still hurt inside, nonetheless. I watched as the zombies began to stir. I was frantic and mad at the same time. I struck a match. It hissed when it was lit.

"No don't do that!" one of them yelled frantically at me.

I looked at my mom and said. "I'm so sorry. I have to do this." I dropped the match on the gas trail, igniting it. I watched as the fire made its way towards the zombies, circling them and keeping them away from me. A few of them tried to cross the angry flames, but their bodies caught on fire. They screamed loudly in pain and fell on the pavement.

All I could hear were screams of anguish, and I turned away leaving them behind me. I was having a hard time keeping it together at this point. For all, I know my mother was burning in the fire I had just lit. I tried not to let the picture of her consume my mind, but I couldn't shake it. I had to slow down and collect myself. Samhain said people don't usually pass the second test. Now I see why. He uses your loved ones against you like he was using my parents.

Remember Brendan, this isn't your world. Your parents are fine. They're not really zombies. This isn't real, it's just a test you have to pass. So far, I felt like I was winning.

Without even realizing it, I came up to Derek's house. I could hide there I thought. The square windows were boarded up and the door was locked. I started to pull off a couple of boards, but they were nailed tight. Finally, one broke loose. I just had to break the other three boards and I would be home free. I started pulling on the other board and it finally broke, and then the third board gave way. The windows were locked so I stepped back and used the chain to break the glass. I watched as the glass shattered into small pieces. I set my scythe and skateboard in through the window, and then slowly climbed inside, trying not to cut myself. I made it. I opened the front door, grabbed the boards I had broken, and tried to cover up the window so that the zombies wouldn't notice that the house had been broken into.

Feeling like I had done my best, I walked back inside Derek's house and locked it. I felt safe. The roof had caved in, there was tile scattered on the floor, and the house smelled worse than a litter box. Derek's living room had too many windows and I didn't want to be seen, so I made my way up the stairs, walking carefully so I wouldn't fall through them like I nearly did at my house. The steps were solid. They weren't loose nor did they creak under my feet. I walked towards Derek's room. I would be safe there. It was at the back of the house and it only had one window through which you could barely see their backyard, so I wasn't too worried about being spotted in his bedroom. I opened the door slowly. Nobody was in there. A sense of relief filled me. I plopped down on the floor and put my head between my hands and tears filled my eyes. I was exhausted, sore and I felt defeated.

A hand shot out from underneath the bed and grabbed me by my ankle. I pulled away quickly and watched as the figure crawled out from underneath the shadows of the bed and into the light. His skin looked green and he wore a torn Star Wars shirt that said Return of the Jedi. I knew who it was. I knew as soon as I saw the shirt. It was Derek. He loved Star Wars and the shirt he was wearing was his favorite. His dad got it for him a couple of years ago before he died in a car accident.

"Brendan, is that you? What are you doing here old buddy? I haven't seen you in years." He said to me.

I didn't have a reply. I watched him for a moment as he started sniffing the air. "Brendan how come you don't smell like one of us? You smell like a human—a living human." He hissed at me.

"You're still alive, aren't you Brendan? Well, that's good. That's really good for me," he said.

"Derek please don't do this. I don't want to hurt you. You're my best friend." I pleaded with him. Derek darted towards me. He was quick. I sidestepped him and watched as he went through the window. He bounced on the shingles twice and then rolled towards the edge of the roof. He caught himself with one hand and he tried to pull himself back up, but I couldn't let him. I climbed out the window and stepped carefully onto the roof of Derek's house.

"Help me, Brendan! Please don't let me fall, you know I hate heights!"

"Derek I'm sorry, but I can't help you up. You will try to hurt me again, and I can't allow it. I stomped on his fingers and heard a loud 'pop 'as the heel of my shoe landed on them. Derek screamed in pain and fell onto the hard-concrete slab of the patio. He hit with a hard thud. Derek didn't move. I watched him for another minute just to make sure. Now I've hurt my best friend, and possibly also my mother. I went back inside the house feeling certain Derek wasn't getting back up. I sat down in Derek's computer chair and I don't even remember falling asleep.

CHAPTER 7

I awoke suddenly to a crow that was standing on the windowsill chirping at me. I grabbed a piece of broken glass and hurled it at the animal. I hit it and it took off. Was I still in the post-zombie apocalypse? I wiped the sleep from my eyes so I could focus.

Yes, I was still in Derek's room. I climbed out on the roof again and Derek was still lying where I left him. There were a couple of crows picking at him. That's just disgusting! I couldn't tell what time it was, or how long I had been out. The sky still looked the same bright orange and red with ash falling everywhere. I went back inside and tried to figure out what to do. I didn't understand. I'd defeated the heard of zombies and defeated Derek. What else did I have to do? I decided it was time to leave Derek's house and figure out what was next.

I made my way to the front door and cracked it open. I peeked outside just to make sure it was safe. If it wasn't, then I would stay inside until I knew I could escape without being caught. I didn't see anything or anyone. The roads were clear. I didn't even hear the wind. I don't even think I've felt the wind the whole time I've been stuck in this world. Here goes nothing I thought as I edged slowly out the door... I had my skateboard in my left hand and my scythe in my right. My clothes were soaked in sweat from the humidity. I carefully walked down the steps, shifting my weight so the boards wouldn't creak under my feet. I wasn't even sure which way I wanted to go. The road was open. I decided I didn't want to go back to where I'd lit the zombies on fire, so I went left.

I tried to think of what my next move would be, but to be honest, I couldn't come up with anything. Did I have to defeat every zombie I came across? Surely not. I tried not to think about what could be happening to Emma. When I last saw her with Samhain, she seemed unharmed. I tried to keep reassuring myself. Samhain said he would be watching. What did that mean? Was he here right now? Is this the third test, and would I face him right now? Questions flooded my mind with no answers to be given. Instead of skating, I decided to walk for a minute. My body felt refreshed from the nap I had taken in Derek's home. I was still sore in some places, but I didn't let it affect me.

Where could I go?

"Samhain I hope you're paying attention! If my count is right, I'm winning!" I announced.

No response. The block was quiet as a cemetery. I decided I would go to my house and see if Samhain was there waiting. I started walking. It would take about fifteen minutes for me to get there from where I was, and I didn't want to get into too much of a hurry. I needed to conserve my strength for whatever came next, so I had to be patient, which was something I don't practice very well, but what kid my age does? I made the block, passed by the elementary school, and stopped in shock at what I saw.

The playground was completely destroyed. The monkey bars were toppled over and some of the bars bent. Whatever bent those bars had to be strong. The roof of the school was caved in, and the door that leads back into the lunchroom from outback was broken in half. The swing sets and merry-go-rounds were all broken, and the basketball goals were bent in half. I was so tired of being here. All I've seen is destruction.

I took another glance at the playground I grew up playing on. There were so many memories about playing basketball or red rover. Now it was destroyed. It looked like a place a ghost hunter would love to go investigate. I continued down the road with barely an upward glance and I heard someone talking within the distance. I kneeled behind the nearest pine tree and looked towards the sound of the voices. It was my father talking with other zombies. I was almost certain they were looking for me. I kept quiet and just listened, trying to hear their conversation.

"We need to find my son and hold him accountable for his actions. He destroyed some of our people and he needs to pay for it." My dad said.

There were about eight zombies altogether, including my dad. If I could defeat twenty zombies earlier, I could stop seven and my dad if I had to. I had the idea to lead the zombies to the dump. I could crush them in the compactor there if necessary.

"Hey, deadheads I'm right here come and get me if you can," I shouted towards their direction. The zombies turned and looked in my direction. My father was standing in the middle like he was the ringleader.

"Didn't you hear me? I said come and get me you deadheads! I'm right here! Aren't you hungry?"

I watched as my father pointed his finger at me, and three of the eight started running towards me. I could take three of them I thought confidently. If I stopped these three, it would give the others the motivation to come after me and do what they could to stop me. I grabbed my scythe and placed the chain I'd acquired on the ground and waited. I didn't feel like running, but I was ready for whatever happened next. The first zombie, who was very tall and skinny, lunged at me hard. I hit him in his solar plexus and watched as he dropped to the pavement. The other two-one that was jolly like Santa Clause and the other a normal size build like me-tried to surround me. I hit big boy across the face with the handle of my scythe, knocking his teeth out. Crack!

He stepped backward and I hit him again, this time on top of his head. Crack! I split his head open and he fell onto the pavement holding his wounded head. The third one caught me by surprise. He grabbed me from behind. I tried breaking his grip, but he was strong. I stomped on his foot. That loosened his grip. I gave him a quick head butt and we both fell on the ground. I scrambled to get up before he did. I kicked him hard in the face and I heard his jaw break. He lay flat on the pavement face down. I planted the top of my foot onto the back of his head and pressed down. I heard bones break. I did the same to the other two for good measure.

"Is that all you got? I beat them! All three of them. Come and get me, Dad! You always told me you could beat me, now's your chance to do it. I know you know I hurt mom in the fire earlier. Why don't you come and do something about it?"

There was a pause then my father screamed at me. "Brendan! I'm going to slowly tear the flesh from your bones and I'm going to do it all by myself! This is the last time you will ever hurt this family! You're a terrible son, boy!"

I knew he didn't mean it because this wasn't really my dad. This was a trick being played on me. Samhain was testing my emotions. This is his game, and it's wrong. Once I beat this test then I planned to beat Mr. Halloween himself, and I looked forward to the fight. But first, it was time to waste some zombies. The rest of the zombies came chasing after me. I hopped on my board and took off. I was about five blocks from Mickey's dump. There I could hopefully lure these guys in and use the compactor on them. It was an idea. I had a little bit of a lead this time, so I kept going using my right leg to gain some speed. I turned and looked behind me. One of the other zombies tripped on the fat one I'd defeated in my brawl earlier.

"Good job! You tripped on your friend's lifeless corpse." I laughed. It seemed to make him even angrier, which is what I wanted. I wanted them to chase me with all they had. Even my own father, or the zombie who resembled my father.

“Get him! Get him!” I heard them shout behind me.

I leapt over a car with my board and watched as one of the zombies ran right into the driver's side door, his head going through the window. These zombies are idiots. They can run fast but they have no intelligence. “You gotta do better than that if you're going to catch me,” I called back to them. I had about three blocks to go and I would be at the dump. I could make it, I assured myself. I could still hear the zombies running behind me. I'm not sure if it was through pure will or not, but I was able to maintain the lead on them. Good, I passed Baker Street. I was getting closer.

“Get him you, idiots! He's just a punk teenage kid. Are you telling me you can't catch him?” my father shouted angrily.

I didn't stop. I had to give it everything I had. I was ready to get out of this world and back to reality.

I could see the dump up ahead. I was so close. The sight of it made me more determined to get there. I tried to skate faster and pick up speed. My hopes were high, and I caught a surge of adrenaline. Now I just had to put my plan into motion. As I got closer, I noticed the gate was unlocked and I was so glad.
Normally, Mickey kept the gate locked with a chain so no one could break in and try to steal from him. I made it through the entrance and dodged the cars so I wouldn't slow myself down. I edged closer to the compactor. All I had to do was make it to the other side and push the button when they fell inside. What I didn't see was the zombie I collided with at the front of the compactor.

We both fell in. I had only a matter of seconds. Suddenly, a sharp pain exploded across my arm. The zombie had bit me across my forearm, although the wound wasn't deep. I grabbed the chain and wrapped it around his neck, choking him. I pulled the chain harder so it would tighten even more around his neck. I could hear the zombie gurgling until it finally passed out.

I had to climb out before they caught up to me and squashed me like a frog. I hurried to the top trying not to drop my belongings. I left the chain. I couldn't carry it with my skateboard and scythe in one hand. I did it! I reached the top and ran to the edge on the other side. I could jump to the ground if I had to. I stood on the metal platform above the compactor and held the controller nervously in my hand. I only hoped my plan would work. I watched as the other five zombies made their way towards me.

They were running so fast. A smile spread across my face. All the zombies but one hadn't realized they were going too fast to slow down before they reached the compactor. Four out of the five fell in. It didn't matter. I went ahead and pressed the green button.

The machine growled to life. I l watched as the remaining four zombies were squashed like tomatoes between the unforgiving walls that pushed them all the way to the back. They tried to escape, but it was useless. I turned and looked at the remaining zombie. My father. He had enough time to slow down before the others fell to their fate.

"Son, it wasn't supposed to be this way. Now, look what you've done. You always ruin everything! You've always been such a spoiled brat!" my father yelled at me.

"I'm not your son and you're not my father! You just look like him but you're not him at all. My father may get frustrated at me, but he would never say anything like you just did!" I yelled back angrily at the slimy thing.

That's it, I was done talking to this thing. I knew it wasn't real. Samhain was using it against me. I climbed down from the platform, ready to face this zombie who looked like my dad. I tightened my grip on my scythe. Once I reached striking distance, I took a hard swing, hitting it in the knee. The zombie cried out in pain.

"Brendan why would you do that I'm your dad1" It cried.

"No, you're not! You're just a zombie that looks like my dad."

I went for another swing and this time I hit my target right across its back. I could hear bones break. The zombie lay flat trying to lift itself up. I hovered over it. For a brief moment, I felt sorry for it. I couldn't let that stop me. I knew what I was going to do to finish him. I was going to put him in the compactor like I did the others. I grabbed him by his injured leg and started to drag him across the ground.

"Brendan, stop! Think about what you are doing. Are you really going to place your dad in the compactor?"

I didn't stop, I just kept dragging him as he shouted at me, pleading with me to stop. I reached the compactor looked inside. The other zombies looked like yesterday's spaghetti.

"Brendan, stop! You'll regret this!"

"No, I won't," I answered. I threw him in without even a second thought. He tried to stand again to get out. I grabbed the controller and looked down at him.

"You're not my father!" I screamed as I hit the green button again. I didn't watch. I just turned my back as the zombie began to scream. I walked out of Mickey's. I had completed my second test. I won again.

"Samhain here I am! I won again!" I cried out.

Then I blacked out again.

CHAPTER 8

I awoke the same way I did the first time like I was falling, and there I laid at Samhain's feet. I looked up at him with a big smile on my face. I hope he'd heard me, and I hoped he was paying attention. I was winning, and since I couldn't see his face, I couldn't tell if he was frustrated or not. "Well, Samhain, I did it again. I won," I announced to him.

"Yes, Brendan, you did. You won again, but you almost lost. There was a point in that test where you wanted to give up. I almost had you. It doesn't matter, you will not win this go around." He answered back to me.

I brushed myself off and looked at Emma. "Are you ok?" I asked her.

"I'm fine Brendan! You did it though you won the second test. Just win this third one and we can go home to mom and dad." I nodded in assurance and stared back at Samhain. I was more than ready for the third test.

"Brendan, I must confess, it's been almost a hundred years since a kid has challenged me. I'm looking forward to this one. You didn't disappoint at all. I'm interested in how well you're going to do."

"So quit talking and let's get on with it, Mr. Halloween. I'm ready to go home."

"You're not going home, Brendan. You and your sister are going to stay with me forever."

"No, we're not, Samhain. I already told you not to underestimate me, and that's what you keep doing. You may have beaten a lot of other kids, but not this time. I don't know how yet, but I'm going to be the first kid to beat you. I just need to figure out your weakness." I replied.

"Brendan you just answered your own question to the puzzle. I have no weakness. There's nothing you can do to defeat me or stop me. Others have already tried, and they failed miserably. But as I said, it will be interesting to watch what you do."

"Then let's get on with it, and we'll see just how invincible you think you are."

"Oh, and there's just one more thing Brendan…I'm going to let your brat sister go. She's going to assist you in this one. So, it will be one of two things. Either she will just be in the way, or she'll be helpful. I'll leave that for you to decide."

I watched as one of the spirits cut the ties from Emma's hands and set her free. She ran over towards me and grabbed me by the hand.

"Brendan, we got this. We can beat him together!" She said confidently.

"Well, Samhain, we're ready when you are," I said. Then we disappeared together.

CHAPTER 9

I awoke in my bedroom laying on my bed just as I did when I faced Buster. This time it was going to be different. I was going to face Mr. Halloween. Where is he? I thought. I stood up and got myself ready to do battle.

He did have me at a slight disadvantage. First, he's letting Emma help me, and second, he's been doing this a long time and hasn't lost yet. My first thought was where's Emma? Did he really bring her back to this world, and what did he do with her? I decided there was no time to waste and started to look for her throughout the house.

I opened my bedroom door and started to look around. "Emma, are you in there?" I called out.
"I'm in my room Brendan! The door is jammed, and I can't open it. Would you see if you can?" She yelled from across the hall. I made my way to her door and tried to turn the knob. Yep, it was jammed alright.

"Emma, stand back. I'm gonna try to kick the door open, ok? I don't want you to get hit if I succeed."

"Ok, I'm standing back. Go for it, Brendan!"

I kicked hard with my right leg. The door barely budged. I kicked a couple more times, but the door wasn't opening. "Emma! Stand as far back as you can. I'm gonna try something dangerous and probably stupid. I'm going to get a running start and throw my shoulder into it and see if that works so I can get you out of there."

"Ok, I'm as far back as I can go. Go for it."

Here goes nothing...I took a few steps back and took in a couple of deep breaths. I started running and propelled my weight into my shoulder hitting the door. It crashed open and I fell face-first onto my sister's kitty rug. If anything, Emma got a good laugh out of the deal watching my face plant into her floor rug. I stood up half embarrassed.

"Nice job brother! That's what you get for trying to be all macho. You got a face full of kitten." Emma teased.

"Emma, we don't have time for this nonsense. We need to find Samhain and defeat him so we can get home safely." I snapped.

Emma didn't say anything. I shouldn't have blown up at her like that. She didn't deserve it. I knew she wanted to be out of here as much as I did. "Emma, I'm sorry. I just want to get us home and go to bed. I'm tired, and I've had enough for one night."

"It's ok, Brendan, I know you didn't mean it. I want out of this just as much as you do."

"Emma, I'm sorry. I shouldn't have made you go with me to the theater. If I hadn't taken us there, we wouldn't be in this mess. We'd be home with mom and we would talk to dad in the morning like we always do when he's away." I said. "You forgive me, sis?" I asked her.

Emma just hugged me, and a tear rolled down her cheek. I got my answer and we walked downstairs. I was curious about what it was going to look like outside. Would it be the zombie apocalypse? Or, would it be just empty houses with no decorations or signs of life? I wasn't in too big of a hurry to find out.

"Emma, you need to grab something to defend yourself with."
"Brendan, I don't know what to grab."

"Go get the baseball bat that dad keeps by the lampshade in the living room. You know which one I'm talking about, the wooden Louisville slugger." I watched Emma run across the living room and retrieve the bat. She looked confident as she made her way back beside me to the front door.

"Ok, Emma listen, and I mean listen. No matter what we face, if it comes at you, you need to hit it as hard as you can. When you swing, you need to swing with everything you've got. Whatever he sends-himself or something else- it's not going to be good." I told her. I opened the front door and it creaked just a little.

We made our way outside, and I couldn't believe what I was seeing. The houses were decorated just like they were before we left to go to our school this afternoon. Pumpkins were still lit with candles. The witch was still crashed face-first into the telephone pole. The scarecrow was still staring at us from across the street. Ok, so are we really home? I thought.

I grabbed Emma by the shoulders and knelt facing her. "Emma, you've got to listen to me. What you see right now looks like home, but it's not, ok? I'm not sure what this place is, but it's not our home and it never will be. Samhain likes to use our emotions and things we care about against us. If we're going to win, we have to realize we're in his world and not ours or what we want it to be. Do you understand?" I asked her.

"I understand Brendan. This place it's not our home, even if it looks like it."

Emma was shaken. I knew she was scared. I had to be brave. I had to be her big brother who wasn't scared. Even if I was, I couldn't let her see it. I had to play the role of the bully. The kid who was always getting into trouble, the kid who tormented others who were smaller than him. That's the big brother I had to be to protect Emma tonight and to ensure we got home. Samhain chose me. Well, he picked the wrong twelve-year-old. I stood out in the middle of the road, the moons bright light shone on Emma and me.

"Come on, Samhain, we're right here waiting! Where are you, you overgrown bat!" I shouted as loud as I could.

"Brendan, over here! Brendan, look over here!" Emma called out to me. I turned and looked at her. She was pointing at something in the sky. I ran towards her and followed her gaze. There in the sky was Samhain. The silhouette of his wings blocked out the moon. He was still huge. He started flying in our direction, coming directly towards us from the sky. Emma raised her bat. We were ready to stand our ground together. Even if we lost, we were going down fighting, and I didn't plan on making it easy. We watched as Samhain landed about forty feet from where we were standing. He folded his wings across his back. They looked kind of like a superhero cape like you would see on T.V.

His red hooded outfit glowed in the moonlight. His eyes looked more menacing than the last time.

"So, it's come down to this, Brendan, just the three of us. I think I made the right choice with you tonight. You're not weak and pathetic like other kids. You're a survivor and a thinker. This should prove interesting. I want you to know I'm going to enjoy this, and I plan on taking my time with you." Samhain spoke directly to me.

I grabbed Emma and shielded her right behind me. "I wish you would just quit talking. You talk too much. I didn't come here to listen to you gloat about yourself, you overgrown bat. I mean, look at you. You're mad at the world because everyone forgot about you, so you take out your frustration on kids. I told you once I'm not afraid of you and that I'm going to beat you."

He didn't say anything. Instead, he lifted his right hand up and lifted it to the sky. I didn't know what to expect. The ground shook beneath our feet like an earthquake. I used my scythe to keep my balance, and Emma was pulling on my shoulder trying to hang on. I watched as a line split through the earth, opening up in the middle of the street. What's going on? I thought to myself.

Samhain's laugh echoed around us. I kept my eyes on the opening in the middle of the street and waited for what was to come next. My right fist clenched tightly, and my brow was covered with sweat. I bent my knees, ready and waiting. I watched as a giant hand came up from the ground, followed by a loud moan. Something or someone was waking up. Another hand emerged, and then its head. His head was dark green with snot running down his nostrils onto his big chest. His eyes were yellow. He had a gold earring dangling in his left ear. He bore a large club in his left hand. I knew what I was looking at now and it was unbelievable! It was an ogre!

"Emma, are you afraid of ogres?" I asked her.

"Yes, just a little! They're so hideous and they eat children! Haven't you read about them, Brendan? Ogres are in all the mythology books." She answered.

I caught onto the game now. Samhain was using Emma's fears against us. The first test was an Ogre. The ogre drew closer. He stood about 12 feet tall and his breathing was heavy. To get to Samhain we had to defeat the ogre and anything else he threw at us. How were we going to defeat this guy?

"Brendan, what do we do?" Emma asked nervously.

"We run to get some distance so I can figure out how to stop him," I answered as I grabbed Emma and slung her over my shoulders, and we took off. I had Emma on my back holding her as we rode on my board. It was difficult to hold my balance as we skated downhill. The ogre let out a long angry scream as we took off. I could hear him running.

"Brendan hurry! He's gaining on us and he's gaining on us quick!" Emma screamed into my ear. I
peddled as hard as I could, but with the weight of both of us on the

board, it was difficult to gain speed. I needed an idea, something to slow down the giant snot nose ogre, but what? Come on Brendan, think! So far, you've been winning. You can beat this big ugly thing. I needed to trip it somehow and make him lose his balance.

"Brendan, faster! You've got to go faster!" Emma screamed at me again. I couldn't look back to see how close he was. I was scanning the area looking for something to use to trip him up. I heard a swing.

"Shift left!" Emma shrieked.

I moved to our left and heard a loud thud hit the ground close to us. The ogre screamed again in anger. It had missed its target. "Emma, how do you stop an ogre, any idea what they're afraid of?" I asked her.

"Come on Emma you've got to know something?" I shouted irritated.

"Water, I think they're afraid of a large body of water. Their heavy so they can't swim. Ogres are afraid of drowning." She finally answered. That gave me an idea but first, we had to buy some time.

I heard another loud thud. It had swung its club and missed us again. I stopped and put Emma on the ground. "Emma hurry! We don't have a lot of time. We need to hide for now and get away from it."

We hopped off the board and ran to the nearest house, cutting through the backyard. There was a patio in the back that was surrounded by fencing at the bottom of it. "Emma come on, crawl under the fence." I held the wire up for her as she crawled through hurrying to hide. I put my board and scythe in next and Emma held up the wire the best she could for me. I crawled under and felt the wire of the fence scraping my back. It hurt but I didn't care. I only cared about getting away for now. I got through, slicing a hole in the right leg of my pants in the process.

"Emma, keep quiet. Keep your breaths low and don't say or do anything," I whispered.

The ogre emerged in the backyard after it kicked over the fence. He looked around trying to find us. I was certain we were safe. We were hiding underneath the back of the porch. I had my hand across Emma's mouth to keep her from screaming. She was shaking so hard and I was doing everything I could to try to calm her down. The ogre turned and started looking around the backyard. It lifted the tool shed looking underneath it for us. Well, at least I know it's stupid. There was no way we could hide under the tool shed.

The ogre swung its club in anger and knocked over a pine tree that fell near the porch where we had hunkered down. I felt something tickle the back of my neck. At first, I thought it was a bug, but when I looked behind me, I couldn't have been any happier. It was an air vent. There was a draft coming from it. I tapped Emma on the shoulder and pointed at the vent. We both started pulling on the metal cover, and it finally gave way so we could crawl through it. I let Emma go in first and then I followed her.

The vent lead us to a basement. Inside were different types of tools, a power saw, split maul, an ax, log chains and a scythe that resembled mine. I laid my cardboard scythe on the ground and picked up the real one... I looked at Emma with a giant smirk on my face. She knew what I was thinking. "I'm taking this," I said. Emma didn't argue. I found a string dangling from the ceiling and pulled on it to turn on the light. I didn't see any windows, so I didn't have to worry about the ogre finding us in here.

"Ok, brat, I have a plan. We can make our way to the public pool. It might be deep enough to trap him in it."

"How do you think that will work? Brendan, you saw how large and fast that thing is. I'm too afraid to try." Emma started to cry. I took a deep breath, trying not to be upset with her. I couldn't blame her for being scared. This whole night was crazy. It was definitely a Halloween to remember, that's for sure. I took in a deep breath.

"Emma listen, I've done this twice now. You have to face your fears, that's how this works. You can either run and hide, or you can summon up courage. You need to find a reason to stand up to this thing, or we're going to be stuck here and Samhain's ogre will eventually find us and defeat us."

Emma wiped the tears from her eyes and just shook her head at me. I hoped that my pep talk worked. If not, this was going to take longer than I anticipated. I found a door that I hoped led inside the house we were occupying. I turned the door handle slowly and we slipped in. I didn't turn on any lights. I didn't want to give away our position in case the ogre was still close by looking for us. Then I found the refrigerator in the kitchen and the best idea crossed my mind. Do they have any food?

I opened the door and looked inside and the first thing I saw was a couple of pizza boxes. I opened them up and it was my favorite, pepperoni. There was also some cream soda. I didn't realize how hungry I was until now. I looked at Emma and she was just as excited as I was. I didn't even try to find plates, I just stuck about five slices in the microwave and heated them up. I peered out a window to see if I could see the ogre. He was gone. He kicked over the back fence leading outwards, thank goodness. The microwave dinged, and Emma and I gorged on the pizza and fixed a couple of glasses of the cream soda. The cream soda was refreshing going down the back of my throat. The pizza was good too. I wanted more, but there wasn't any left. I let out a loud belch.

"Uh, Brendan that's gross," Emma muttered.

"No, that's just the sound of success. You know it's customary to burp at the table of some countries, right?" I asked her.

"Only you would know something like that Brendan."

"Ok, Emma we have to defeat this giant Ogre. You said water was its weakness. I bet we can drown him in the water park, and I have an idea on how to do it. We can use the ropes they use to make the lanes that the swim team uses. We'll set them as tripwires for him to fall over so he goes headfirst into the pool. Then hopefully he drowns. If not, we tried. At least it'll slow him down. What do you say?"

Emma was wolfing down another slice of pizza not even paying attention to anything I had just said. "Emma, did you hear me?"

She looked up at me confused. "What'd you say, Brendan?"

"Never mind!" I muttered. Sometimes having a sister can be annoying. This was one of those times, especially since our lives depended on us winning.

"Emma, please focus. I need you to pay attention, Ok? We're going to stop the Ogre. We're going to lure him to the pool at the water park, and I'm gonna make a tripwire with the ropes and use them to trip him up so he will drown. I'll lure him in, and we'll trip him at the right moment."

"Brendan I don't know if I can! I mean, I'm scared," she replied.

"Emma, please, listen. I'll make sure nothing happens to you! You have to trust that I know what I'm doing. For us to get out of this predicament we have to defeat the ogre." I tried to sound enthusiastic. I wasn't sure if it was working or not, but I had to get her to agree with me.

"All right, Brendan, I trust you. You've gotten us this far." She replied.

"Ok then, let's go. The quicker we beat the ogre, the sooner I can figure out a way to beat Samhain and we can go home. Emma took one last drink of her cream soda and we headed outside into the cold air.

CHAPTER 10

We walked out into the cold night air hoping to go unnoticed by the ogre. I wanted the element of surprise as leverage. I couldn't let the big ugly giant catch onto what we were going to do. I just hoped Emma was right and that they were afraid of water. Emma was drinking a soda she had taken out of the refrigerator before we left, and I had grabbed a bottle of water. I felt so dehydrated from everything that's happened up to now.

I hadn't realized that we were passing Mrs. Burnett's home. She was my fourth-grade teacher. She had once told me I was a terror. Her house was large and painted forest green with white shutters. She hated Halloween. Her house wasn't even decorated. I think she hated Christmas too. I always said she would be perfect for Scrooge if he was a real person and not a fictional character. The nickname stuck. Everyone laughed and called her Mrs. Scrooge Bennett the witch.

I got in trouble and sent to the principal's office for telling her that. The principal told me I should respect my elders more, but I think he got a chuckle out of it too. I laughed as we walked by her home thinking about that.

"What's so funny Brendan?" Emma asked me curiously.

"Just thinking about something I did a couple of years ago."

"Like what?"

"It's nothing. Let's just get to the pool and hope this works." I replied. We walked down the street, and I remembered a shortcut to the pool.

"Emma, we're going to take a shortcut I know about through the cemetery," I told her. She stopped in her tracks.

"Emma it's just a graveyard. There's nothing to worry about. We'll get there a lot quicker and there's less of a chance we'll run into the ogre that's hunting us," I stated.

"You don't know if it's safe! Think about where you're talking about going! A graveyard. It's also Halloween! Have you forgotten about the current position we're in because of you? You had to go into the old theater! We would be home right now if you hadn't wanted to go in there!" She screamed at me.

"Look, I know I messed up, but we can't fix that now. We have to work together to get out of here. The longer we stand around here arguing about it, the longer it takes for us to get back home to mom and dad. So, I really need you to get on board with what's going on so we can do this and get out of here okay!"

"Fine, you win Brendan. You're always right and I'm just the brat sister that doesn't know anything. We'll do it your way and see how it works out. You want to walk through creepy graveyards. Fine, I'll walk through the creepy graveyard with you."

We came upon the entrance to the graveyard. The cast-iron gate clanged shut, echoing throughout the graveyard. I grabbed the handle to pull it back open. It was ice cold to the touch. I pulled and the gate opened with ease.

"Come on hurry up," I said to Emma.

We walked inside the cemetery and I shut the gate as quietly as I could, careful not to draw attention to ourselves. We walked along the concrete path and I gazed at the tombstones, thinking that could be me in the next couple of minutes if I lost. I shuddered at the thought of it. Emma seized my arm. She was still terrified.

"I had to come out here and do some rubbings a couple of weeks ago for a class," Emma spoke up. "I didn't enjoy it. This place has always creeped me out. I don't understand why people find graveyards and rubbings so fascinating."

"I don't know, think about it. Some of these people might have actually had an awesome life. I mean, if you could somehow talk to them and listen to their life story, what do you think they'd have to say to us." I responded.

She looked at me with a frown and groaned. She was tired, but so was I. We kept moving forward. We passed one large mausoleum that had an archangel standing at the top of it. It was for a wealthy family that was buried together. Supposedly, they died in their sleep when their house caught on fire.

They were the Stevens family. They owned a large shoe factory downtown and employed many people. Rumor is their ghosts still haunt the land where the house burned down. They say you can hear the kids screaming for help at night. A cold chill raced down my spine at the thought of it.

Derek told me he had checked it out one night by himself. He told me how big their land was, and about the large pond that was in the backyard with a dock they used for swimming. He said there was a substantial stable on the west end where they kept their horses. Now it's about to collapse and fall to pieces. He said that some of the brick from the homestead was still standing, but there was not much of it left. Derek told me he took a brick home with him. He thought it was cool. I guess it gave him bragging rights.

One night he said he saw the ghost of the little girl Gabriel down by the stables, supposedly she was looking for her horses. When she turned and looked at Derek, she screamed. Derek said she disappeared before his eyes like a vapor--there for a second then, just gone. I wasn't sure if I believed him or not. I know how much

Derek likes to build himself up, but who knows, he might be telling the truth. If I survive this, I might go check out the Steven's land myself just to see what happens I thought.

We were halfway through the cemetery. Once we reach the east end, we can hop the fence, which will take us straight to the pool. A sense of relief filled me, but it was short-lived because that's when I saw the skeletons, and they started charging towards Emma and me. I took in a deep breath and tried to grasp what I was seeing. There were three skeletons running towards us. "Emma get behind me! If they get me, you run and hide," I told her.

Emma ducked behind me, and I stood ready. Here I go again, another fight on my hands. I clenched my scythe and took a swing at the first skeleton, hitting him in the ribs and knocking him to the ground. The other two skeletons grabbed my arms and began trying to pry my weapon out of my hands. Suddenly the skeleton on my right side lost his head, literally, its head went flying off its shoulders. The other one was still clenching my left hand tightly. I punched it in the face with my right hand. It was a bad idea because it hurt, but at least I'd knocked it off balance. Emma took her bat and crushed his head in. Pieces of his skull fell everywhere.

"Not bad, Emma seems the bat suits you."

"Yeah, you know, I got my swing playing softball." She smirked at me.

I was happy she had a little bit more confidence in herself. We pressed on. I didn't want any more distractions. We came to the east end where all the old tombstones were. Some of the tombstones were faded by the acid rain. You couldn't even make out the names on them, or the years. Mom told me that the town's founding families were buried here, but there was no historical record of it. We made it to the back end and climbed the stone wall. I toppled over with ease. Emma, on the other hand, struggled due to her height and not being very strong. When she came down, I barely caught her. I sat her down and she brushed herself off.

“I ripped my dress.” She whined.

“Emma we’ve got bigger problems to worry about. I’m sure I can sew it back together once we make it home.” I tried to reassure her. “We’re almost there,” I told her.

We walked in silence down the dirt path that led to Abraham Street where the pool was. I heard an owl and some bats in the distance. They didn’t bother me, honestly. I love being in the woods and around nature, it was like a second home to me. After a few minutes we came to the end of the path and walked out onto Abraham Street.

The pool area looked creepy at night. We made our way around back and I found the Olympic ropes and looked for a good place to tie them to trip the ogre when he came for us. I took one end and tied it tightly around a pine tree and the other around the gated fence. I pulled both ends as tight as I could. I looked over into the pool and saw that it was covered by a tarp. That was even better.

I took my scythe and poked a couple of holes in it to let the water rise to the top. If this thing truly couldn’t swim and was afraid of water the tarp could help suffocate it. Now we just had to lure it in, but how?

“Emma, how can we lure the ogre in?” I asked her.

She opened her mouth to stay something and before she could, I heard loud footsteps in the distance. I didn’t need to lure him in, after all, he was making his way here. “Emma, go hide, I got this,” I whispered to her. Emma ducked under one of the tables that were sheltered by the surrounding pine trees. I made my way slowly to the front entrance and looked down the street. He was coming my direction with his club still in hand. Here goes nothing.

“Hey you big, snot-nosed, ugly ogre! I’m over here! Come and get me, you big idiot."

The ogre screamed and then charged at me. I waited a couple of seconds for it to get closer and then I started to run to where the tripwire was. I hopped over it and slid to my left, crashing into a table and chairs. I watched as the ogre tripped on the rope and fell forward, skidding across the concrete into the pool. When he fell, I heard one of his legs break. The ogre screamed and splashed around trying to pull himself up out of the pool. He couldn't do it. He wasn't strong enough to lift his own weight. The tarp was wrapped around his head and he was fighting to lift it off. The ogre tried again to lift himself up out of the pool. Emma came running up behind me with her bat and started to hit the ogre's hands, breaking his fingers. The ogre screamed again in pain.

The ogre was swinging wildly trying to lift the tarp off his head, but he couldn't get a grip on it because Emma had broken all his fingers. We did it! We trapped the ogre, and we're about to defeat him. The ogre thrashed and screamed for a couple of more minutes. He was scared. Suddenly, he stopped, his breathing labored. The ogre took a couple more breaths and collapsed hard into the pool without even moving. He gave up. He knew he couldn't get out, so he just quit. Emma shouted in victory, "Brendan you did it! We defeated the ogre!"

We celebrated our victory for a moment as we walked out of the pool area and left Abraham Street behind us. I wasn't sure where we were going, and it didn't matter. I knew it was only a matter of minutes, maybe even moments, before Samhain would appear to us again and the final fight would take place.

We came to an intersection between Grand and Baker Streets. There before us stood Samhain with his arms crossed patiently waiting on us as we edged closer. My stomach lurched nervously. This was the moment, and what I did next, even I stood in disbelief.

CHAPTER 11

I threw my scythe as hard as I could. I watched as it spun towards Samhain, hitting my target. The scythe hit him in the side of his face, leaving a small gash. Samhain flinched. He took his left hand and wiped the side of his face. A drop of blood trickled down his left index finger then he turned and stared at me coldly.

"I told you I wasn't afraid of you." I boasted.

"Then that will be your downfall, Brendan!"

"Emma, run! Find a hiding spot!" I yelled at her.

Emma ran to the nearest house and hid under the porch. I grabbed my skateboard and, skated forward to pick up my scythe. Samhain spread his wings and lifted himself up high above the ground. I grabbed my weapon and started to pick up speed. My plan was to get Samhain as far away from Emma as I could, so I had to keep him focused on me until I found a way to defeat him. I looked back over my shoulder. He was gaining on me fast. There was no way I could outrun him. I took a hard right and he barely missed me. I turned to look behind me. As I watched, his wing clipped the side of a house, knocking out the side and collapsing the roof. For the first time, I thought to myself that I could be in over my head.

Samhain turned and came at me for a second time. I threw my scythe hard at him once again. He covered his face with his wings. My weapon struck his left-wing, ripping it. That's twice I've gotten the best of him.

"Brendan, now your mine!" he screamed.

"Yeah? You gotta catch me first and so far, you're not doing a very good job of it."

I kept skating down the street trying to gain momentum to get a good lead. I looked over my shoulder and Samhain was still flying towards me. This game of cat and mouse wasn't going to work. Eventually, I would get tired and wear out. I had to figure out another way to slow him down or I had to hide until I could come up with a way to beat him.

I hooked a sharp left on my board, and I felt an intense pain in my back. I lost my balance and collided into some garbage cans and rolled across the grass. I was happy to hit the ground because it was soft, so it didn't hurt too bad. I felt my back. My skin was cut open. He scratched me! I looked up and saw him turning around high in the sky to come at me again, I got up and threw my board and weapon into the backyard. I was climbing the top of the fence when Samhain came barreling through the middle of the house, shattering it into pieces.

It sounded like a bomb going off. Bricks went everywhere! The fence collapsed on top of me, trapping my left leg. I tried to pull it out as hard as I could, but I was stuck. Great. All this work leading up to this one moment, and now I was done for. I watched as Samhain emerged from the dust of the house and glared down at me. I tried with all my might to pull myself free but, I couldn't. I was unable to move.

"Well, Brendan, it would seem your arrogance has finally caught up with you. You're trapped like the scared little rat you are."

This was it; I'm done for. Just when I was ready to give up hope, out of the corner of my eye I saw Emma. She was climbing the one pine tree Samhain didn't knock down when he crashed through the house. She edged herself out onto a limb, keeping her balance. She lifted her bat high above her head and took a giant leap onto Samhain's head. "You leave my big brother alone!" She screamed.

She hit him in the back of the head, jumped off his back, and raced to me. Samhain shrieked in pain as he fell to one knee.

"Brendan get up hurry get up!"

"I can't my legs caught under the fence. You're going to have to help me lift it." I told her. Emma grabbed the fence and started to lift with everything she had. I was able to wiggle free. My leg was significantly scraped, but it wasn't cut like I thought it would be.

"I thought I told you to hide Emma."

"Well, gee, you're welcome, and you did tell me to hide. I just didn't listen. I guess I get that from you," She smirked at me.

I grabbed her as we raced out of the yard. I had my board and weapon in hand. Samhain was starting to recover. "Get to the woods! He can't find us there," I shouted. We crossed Baker Street into the wood line. The woods were thick, and he'd have a hard time finding us in there as long as we stayed quiet. I wasn't paying attention and walked straight into a thorn briar bush. I hate those things. I found us some cover in a thick brush and motioned for Emma to stay quiet. I looked up as Samhain was flying overhead looking for us. I prayed feverishly that he didn't see us. He circled a couple more times and then shouted. "I will find you! You two will not escape me! I will find a way to make you come out of hiding!"

"Emma what were you thinking? You could have gotten yourself hurt, or worse," I told her, "but I'm glad you showed up when you did because I was about to be done for!"

"Well, yeah, I sure saved your butt, didn't I? Ole' big bad Brendan about got his butt handed to him by Samhain. I guess you owe me one, don't you?" She teased.

I gave her a stern look and she stuck her tongue out at me. There was no way I was going to give her the satisfaction of knowing that for once in my life I needed her. Nope, not me. Not going to do it.

"Whatever think what you want. I was doing just fine."

Emma started laughing uncontrollably. "Oh, come on, Brendan, does the fact that you actually needed your sister to save you because you were losing hurt your pride that bad?"

"Ok! Ok! Thank you. But, you're still a brat." I chuckled.

Emma didn't find my joke funny. She knew there was no way I was going to admit that I needed her help, even if it was true. Not that I'm not grateful or anything, but I have a reputation to uphold and a spirit to figure out how to beat. "Brat, all jokes aside, we need to figure out how to beat Samhain. We've injured him a couple of times, now we need to figure out how to finish him and I'm not even sure what his weakness is. Do you have any ideas?"

Emma thought about it for a moment. She was smart, I'd give her that. For her age she was intelligent, maybe even more intelligent than me, but I wouldn't admit that either. After a few moments, a big smile crossed her face.

"Brendan, I think I've got it! What if we've been going about this the wrong way?"

"What do you mean?" I asked, puzzled by her answer.

"Think about it. When we were back at the theater, Samhain told us how people used to fear him. Years ago, they dressed up in masks to ward off evil spirits. He said the people stopped fearing him, and he stopped existing. So, what if we choose to stop believing in him the way everyone else did? He uses our fears against us, but if we don't believe in him or his tricks, then maybe we can defeat him." She sounded confident.

"Emma, he seems pretty real to me. I mean, come on, I watched him knock over a house like it was nothing. We've both seen what he can do. Are you sure this will work?"

"It has to! He has to exist if we believe in him and fear him. If we no longer fear him, then he doesn't have a hold on us and maybe, just maybe, we can stop him forever and he'll leave us, and all kids alone."

I thought about it for a minute because we couldn't afford to be wrong. It sounded good. I mean, physically, I was losing. He was powerful and the wounds we inflicted on him hadn't seemed to slow him down. "All right Emma, we'll try it your way. I hope it works." I felt like I was in a Scooby-Doo episode and now I was waiting for Emma to say "Jinkies!" now that she'd solved the mystery.

We walked quietly, careful not to snap any twigs so we could proceed undetected. Samhain circled over us one more time. I was confident he couldn't see us due to how thick the pine trees were. His shadow cast over us a couple more times, as we were coming to the edge of the tree line. "Brendan we should wait back here until we're sure he's gone," Emma whispered softly into my ear.

"You're right. We'll stop and wait and see if he gives up," I whispered back to her. I sat down with my back against a tree. I could have gone to sleep I was so tired. Emma sat beside me and rested her head on my shoulder. We enjoyed a few minutes of silence, but I knew we needed to get going. "Emma we've got to go. We've got to get out of here." I told her. She stretched her arms and let out a yawn. I looked up to the sound of trees snapping and falling near us. Samhain had found us.

"Run!" I yelled at Emma.

We made a dash to the tree line as limbs fell around us. I don't know how we didn't get hit by any, except that we must have had dumb luck. Suddenly, Emma screamed, "Brendan he's got me! Brendan, please don't let him take me."

I looked and Samhain had Emma in his left hand. "Brendan you know where I'll be if you want your sister back. I'll be waiting," he said as he spread his long wings, lifted in the air, and took off. All I could hear were Emma's screams in the distance.

I knew where he was going all right. Where it all began, the theater where we first met. I hopped on my skateboard and started to skate towards the theater. I was around five miles away. I pushed on my board as hard as I could. The air was still cool. I tried to ignore it, but it was hard. The temperature felt like it had dropped ten degrees. I had to get there as fast as I could. My sister was depending on me to make it. I only hoped her theory was right. I was going to try it. At this point, I was desperate to try anything.

I arrived at the theater nearly thirty minutes later. My heart was thudding hard in my chest. I stared up at the old building and opened the front door. The theater looked the same as it had earlier, with spider webs everywhere and the smell of mold and dust lingering in the air. I found the door that led towards the stage, opened it, and walked in.

Inside I saw Samhain and all the spirits who did his bidding, They were all sitting in the theater seats. As I entered, they turned towards me, staring at me coldly. I spotted Emma tied up sitting in the same spot she had before. I walked towards the old wooden stage not paying any attention to the spirits that hissed at me as I passed them by. My only focus was now was Emma and getting us back to our home. I walked up the wooden steps and they creaked as they had before. I stood within ten feet of Samhain and stared up at him.

"I see you made it. Brendan, I want you to know it's been a pleasure. You have made tonight interesting, and I must say I've enjoyed myself, but like all things, tonight must come to an end." He spoke.

"You're right, they must. We've been playing this game for a long time now, and it's time you came to your end." I answered him back.

"Brendan, surely you don't think you can defeat me even now?"

"Yes, I do think I can still defeat you. You see, I realized something tonight. You gave yourself away earlier when you introduced yourself to Emma and me when this whole night started. You said you wanted people to start fearing you again because you had been forgotten."

"I think I know what your fear is Samhain. You're afraid you won't exist anymore, which is why you choose to go after kids. Emma pointed that out tonight when you were chasing us. Pretty smart for a brat, isn't she? So now I will say this. It's time you, Samhain, face your fear just as we have."

"Brendan, you are so arrogant! I am a Master of fear! I am the spirit of Halloween! I create fear! I AM fear!" He yelled.

"Not tonight Samhain! You see, I don't fear you and neither does Emma. You can't do anything to us if we no longer fear you, so that means you'll cease to exist."

"Another thing, Samhain, tonight I chose to dress as the grim reaper. I'm sure you know what the reaper represents, so yes, it's time that you meet your end once and for all!"

I pulled my skull mask over my face and I charged violently towards Samhain. I lifted my scythe high above my head and let out a loud scream as I jumped up towards his head. With a giant swing, I cut his head open, and a ray of light came out of it.

Samhain screamed in pain as he fell with a thud onto his back. Flashes of light filled the room as it shook violently. The other spirits that surrounded Emma and I screamed in fear. I grabbed Emma, and we made our way off the stage. Emma tripped on the bottom of the step, and the other spirits surrounded us, not letting us move.

"Get out of the way or I'll do to you what I just did to your master," I shouted.

The spirits recoiled and didn't dare touch us. Emma and I ran out of the theater door and into the main lobby. I didn't care if I ran into spider webs. I wanted out of this theater, and I wanted out now. We made our way out the main entrance and onto the street. We crossed the street and turned and watched as the theater collapsed. We could hear the screams of Samhain and all his spirits who followed him. We watched as the dust settled, and I looked for any kind of movement. There was nothing.

"Brendan you did it! You defeated Samhain!" Emma shouted happily.

"Maybe, but let's not stick around to find out. Let's just go home Emma, it's been a long night." I said.

We turned and walked away from the fallen theater, and I couldn't bring myself to turn and look back again. I just wanted to get home, and for tonight to finally be over with. We walked and turned down our street, and I was never happier to see our home and what was parked out in the front yard. It was mom's car. I wondered what time it was, and if we were going to be in trouble for being out so late. It had to be close to dawn, and I'm sure mom was up waiting for us wondering where we were. I was certain the blame would fall on me since I was the oldest.

We walked up the steps and mom met us at the door. "So, how was the fall festival?" she asked quizzically.

"What do you mean?" I asked her.

"Did you have fun or not is what I mean Brendan. It's not a rhetorical question."

Emma and I looked at each other and answered simultaneously, "It was great."

"Well, come on in. I stopped at the movie rental store and got us a scary movie to watch."

"Mom, what time is it?" I asked.

She looked at her watch and answered. "It's barely ten-thirty. Emma, put your bag of candy on the kitchen table and we'll sort it out in a little bit. I popped some popcorn for us and bought sodas for you two to drink."

Emma looked down, and in her left hand was the bag of candy she had earlier. I thought she had lost it. I also noticed her dress wasn't dirty or ripped. I checked myself over, and in my left hand was my homemade scythe, and my skateboard was by the front door. This was weird. I guess everything was back to normal. I watched Emma put her bag of candy on the kitchen table as mom had instructed. Mom opened the refrigerator, grabbed a couple of sodas, and handed me one.

"Mom, I'm going up to change first, and then I'll be back down," Emma said.

"Go ahead honey. I'm sure you're hot in that dress."

I heard Emma's footsteps as she made her way upstairs to her bedroom. "Brendan, would you please put your skateboard away? That thing makes me nervous looking at it. I'm always afraid you're going to fall one day and break your leg or an arm." My mother asked me.

I grabbed my board and started up the stairs when I heard Emma scream. I rushed up the steps and opened her door, my mom following close behind. I opened her door and saw what had scared her. I forgot I had hidden a skeleton head in her closet on top of her shoe rack. It must have fallen when she opened her closet door.

"Brendan what did your father and I tell you about your pranks?" my mother yelled at me.

"Mom, it's ok. It's kind of funny, and besides, that's just Brendan and I wouldn't ask him to change," Emma spoke softly.

My mom still gave me a stern look as she made her way downstairs. "I'll see you two in a minute." She called back up to us.

"Thanks, Emma."

"It's ok Brendan. Besides, you saved us tonight and so far, things seem to be back to normal."

Emma gave me a hug then she closed her door to change. I made my way towards my room to change as well. I took off my costume and left it on the floor. I was happy to be out of it. I put on some flannel pants and a white t-shirt and made my way downstairs. Emma followed behind me. We sat on the couch and mom handed us our bowls of buttery popcorn. I ate a handful. It was good to be home and in my warm house.

"So, mom, what's the movie about?" I asked.

"It's about a Halloween spirit named Samhain who preys on kids." She answered.

I dropped my bowl of popcorn, spilling it on the living room floor. "Don't watch that! No, we don't need to watch that!" I yelled as she hit the play button.

ABOUT THE AUTHOR

Robert Campbell

Robert was raised in Magnet Cove, AR and currently resides in Hot Springs AR. He is an avid collector of vintage books and all things macabre. He also researches the paranormal in his spare time.

Made in the USA
Coppell, TX
18 September 2020

38250839R00059